I want to say at the outset that I have become ill, insane, as an inmate of the torture chamber behind America's fake facade of justice and democracy. But I am not as ill as I was, and I am getting better all the time.

I want to make clear that my reason for starting these notes at a point of personal anguish and suffering is that these experiences marked the end of a corrupt pimp life and were the prelude to a still mauled but constructive new life.

THE NAKED SOUL OF ICEBERG SLIM

by ROBERT BECK

AN ORIGINAL HOLLOWAY HOUSE EDITION
HOLLOWAY HOUSE PUBLISHING CO.
LOS ANGELES, CALIFORNIA

Standard Book Number 87067-414-5

PUBLISHED BY:
Holloway House Publishing Company
8060 Melrose Avenue
Los Angeles, California 90046

First Printing 1971

Printed in the United States of America

Cover illustration by Earnie Kollar

Design by A. Marshall Licht

I dedicate this book to
the heroic memory of
Malcolm X, Jack Johnson,
Melvin X, Jonathan Jackson;
to Huey P. Newton,
Bobby Seale, Ericka Huggins,
George Jackson, Angela Davis;
and to all street niggers
and strugglers in
and out of the joints.

INTRODUCTION

Robert Beck—or Iceberg Slim as his people know him—is living evidence (for those who need it) that times have not changed—only the con. A century ago, fifty years ago, twenty years ago, the Establishment line was, "Take it easy, don't rock the boat. Justice will come—but it takes time."

Today the con is, "We must have Law and Order. Now civil rights legislation is being passed. Justice will come—but it takes time." (Tomorrow, the con will be something like, "You can't get anything by bloodshed. Take it easy. Justice will come.") The truth is, nothing has changed. The same Establishment against which Jack Johnson fought single handedly (see *The Big Black Fire* by Robert H. deCoy—the only biography of the greatest fighter prior to Muhammed Ali which captures the essence of the man and his times), the same Establishment that murdered Bessie Smith, the same Establishment that murdered Malcolm X and Melvin X—to say nothing of the nameless thousands every year in the collective ghetto of our nation—that is the same Establishment of today—and it hasn't yielded one inch in all this time.

Most of the black writers of this time are screamers—and some are pretty loud. But Iceberg Slim—the greatest story teller of the ghetto—doesn't waste his time. He knows that a black man is something a great deal more than just one of the downtrodden and damned; that every black man carries not only the collective burden of his blackness—but he is also very much an individual human being.

His first book, *Pimp: The Story of My Life,* is essentially a modern and very much American version of *Crime and Punishment.* This is not to suggest a borrowing from or even an influence by Dostoievsky—but it is a very sincere and sometimes frightening attempt on the part of Iceberg Slim to face himself and his life; and his final transformation—or salvation, if you wish—is as intensely meaningful as any religious enlightenment recorded by the saints. In this book you hold in your hand, Iceberg Slim recounts how he happened to write *Pimp*, and why he wrote it himself rather than trust it to another (see "The Professor"). Elsewhere in this group of essays and vignettes you will see the effect that book has had on the black ghetto youth. To many, Slim has become a folk hero and his followers dream of emulating him. They are thrilled with the excitement of the street, and feel strong enough to weather its deadly dangers.

Pimp fast became an underground bestseller—and, now, four years after the first edition, it is still a bestseller (though it will never appear on the Establishment Bestseller List). Iceberg Slim followed with *Trick Baby*, a story of the con game and of a black man so light that he could have passed had he not felt his blackness so strongly (and this was a whole generation before black was beautiful). A small portion of *Trick Baby* is repeated here in "Uncle Tom and his Master in the Violent Seventies." Repeated because it recounts something of the inner workings of the Establishment con—much as John A. Williams revealed it in the King Alfred Plan in *The Man Who Cried I Am* (a book which should be read by every American who is concerned with something more than his income tax).

Iceberg Slim's next book was *Mama Black Widow,* the story of a Southern family which was destroyed when it moved to a Northern city. It is interesting to compare the Tilson family—and Otis Tilson, who tells the story—with James Baldwin's Rufus in *Another Country.* Rufus was utterly destroyed by Whitey—or so Baldwin would have us believe. And there is much pain in the telling. But Otis Tilson tells his story "for my poor dead Papa and myself and the thousands of black men like him in ghetto torture chambers who have been and will be niggerized and deballed by the white power structure and its thrill-kill police. . . ." And if this were all there was to his story, Iceberg would merely be another Baldwin or LeRoi Jones or Julius Lester or the like. But, as mentioned earlier, Iceberg Slim is no screamer—not that he evades issues, by any means. But he is too strong a man and too honest to cop out. A man—whoever he may be—is a great deal more than *just* black or *just* white. Those who, like Baldwin and Lester and the KKK and the FBI, are willing to accept such simplified classifications tend to view the American situation today as a gigantic and very serious game of cops-and-robbers. Such ready-made categories save a lot of wear and tear on the brain cells—but no problems can be solved until they are faced squarely and as free of illusion as possible. This, Iceberg Slim attempts to do in all his writings (as does Robert H. deCoy in *The Nigger Bible,* in his own way and for his own reasons).

Much has been written of late about "the generation gap." This phenomenon which occurs repeatedly throughout history is also very evident among the black generations. Iceberg touches on this in his vignette of "The Black Panthers." "The Panther youngsters," he says, "were blind to my negative glamour and, in fact, expressed a polite disdain for my former profession and its phony flash of big cars, jewelry and clothes. Their only obsession seemed to be the freedom of black people." And he becomes "aware of the fact that Black Panthers are the authentic champions and heroes of the black race, and are as a whole categorically superior to that older generation of physical cowards of which I am a part."

George Jackson, one of the Soledad Brothers, would not be as hard on Slim. "You must stop giving yourself pain by feeling that you failed somehow," he writes to his mother. "You have not failed. You have been failed, by history and events, and people over whom you have no control." (From his letter of March 12, 1965, as published in *Soledad Brother,* Bantam Books, Inc., New York City, 1970.)

And in what is to my mind the high point of this book, "Letter to Papa," Slim remembers his own earlier rejections and denunciations of his own father. But he also remembers this man who was one of "that older generation of physical cowards" in a moment of glory when he single-handedly stood up to the white power structure.

At any rate, in this volume are collected some of the soul searchings of Iceberg Slim. Some are extremely personal, all are extremely honest. In some, the reader will recognize "first attempts" to face a specific situation squarely, and not always with complete success. But the reader can be certain, as am I, that Iceberg Slim will never allow himself to be conned by the easy answers, but will continue his almost ruthless searching of that beautiful soul which is his.

Milton Van Sickle
Los Angeles
February, 1971

FROM A STEEL BOX TO A WICKED YOUNG GIRL

I want to say at the outset that I have become ill, insane as an inmate of a torture chamber behind America's fake facade of justice and democracy. But I am not as ill as I was, and I am getting better all the time. And also, I want to make clear that my reason for starting these notes at a point of personal anguish and suffering is that these experiences marked the end of a corrupt pimp life and were the prelude to a still mauled, but constructive new life. I am not "playing the con" for sympathy.

In the cold-blooded academy of ghetto streets I was taught early that suffering is inevitable and necessary for an aspiring pimp, pickpocket or con man and even just a nigger compelled to become a four-way whore for the Establishment. I learned also that sympathy is a counterfeit emotion for suckers which is usually offered with a crooked con grin of amused contempt and rejected with a spittled snarl.

Within the moldering walls of Chicago's House of Correction, in one of its ancient cellhouses, is a row of steel punishment cubicles where rule-breaking inmates spend at most several days. In 1960 I was locked in one of the steel boxes for ten months. I owed the joint an unserved part of a sentence from which I had vanished thirteen years before like a wisp of black smoke and without the usual damage to joint fixtures or guards' skulls. And apparently the sweet joker who ordered me stuffed into the steel box to commit suicide or go mad (when I was returned to the joint on escape charges) felt he owed vengeance on me to his long-ago fellow clique of torturers and grafters who must have suffered a shit storm of consternation and rage when nigger me bypassed their booming instant release service and hadn't bought out, but thought out.

But that second mob of debonair demons sure butchered off a hunk of my mental ass. For even now, a new life and a decade later, I will lay odds that until the grave the images and sounds of that violent, gibbering year will stomp and shudder my mind.

One instance, among many: I am in a pleasant mood when I hear through an open window the profane chanting of teenagers playing a merry game of ghetto dozens (*dozens*—the denigration of another's parents or ancesters) that explode in a montage of pain, bright as flame, that shocks my brain. Again for the thousandth time I see and hear the likable little black con in the steel box next to mine, my only buddy, suddenly chanting freaky lyrics of a crazy frightening song about how God is a double-crossing cocksucker, and how he is going to sodomize and murder his crippled bitch mama.

I cry out like a scalded child, leap off my straw mattress and stand on trembly legs peering into Shorty's cubicle through a ragged break in the weld of the sheet steel wall. He's buck naked and his soft black baby face is twisted hard and hideously old as he stands slobbery with his hands flying like frenzied bats up and down his long stiff penis.

I have the vague hope that he's "gaming," playing the con, for the heartless white folks for some personal benefit or advantage. But there's a chilling realism, a perfection about

Shorty's awful performance, so I rib him gently.

"Buddy, put your pants on and stop that chump jeffing. (*Jeffing*—playing or employing a low grade of con based on one's blackness and the projection of the contemptible "Sambo" or "Rastus" image.) Instead of a hospital broad tucking you between white sheets, the ass kickers will show any minute now. Dummy up for me, pal. Huh? I like you and I got a weak belly."

Shorty gives me zero response and his walling eyes are like coals of white fire. I feel a jolt of panic in my chest and a terrifying fluttery quaking inside my skull.

And because I know that madness can be catching I get stupid and scream, "You little jive ass, you're suppose to be a player. Remember? What you gonna do, let these dirty white folks crack you up?"

But he's so pitiful I go soft and plead, "Shorty, get your head together. Please pal, listen to me!"

I beg him until I stink of emotion sweat and my voice fades to a squealy whisper. But Shorty doesn't listen for the pathetic reason that he can't hear me or anything else except his private hellish drum beat.

The guards come soon to take Shorty away

forever and he yelps and whimpers like a puppy under their fists and feet. I quiver and my teeth slash into my bottom lip with every thud. And as Shorty is dragged away I sink to the concrete floor and roll myself into a fetal ball against a frightening chaos of pulsing green-streaked puffy bladders that whirl madly in terrible near collision on a shuddery screen inside my head. I feel great anguish and terror as if the berserk missiles are really sections of myself facing bloody destruction.

The tragedy of Shorty and its recurring long range misery for me is but one "House" horror among many that haunt my new life.

A day or so before my expected legal release date from the "House," I was taken from my steel box to an interview with a charmer who told me with a choreographed Billy Graham type smile that a new computation of my time served and owed left me in debt to the joint for two additional months. I had spent the two months in County Jail where I had been taken after Captain Churchill, a "House" bloodhound, backed by city police, crashed my pad and cracked me on an ancient fugitive warrant for the escape from the "House."

I had expected the attempt to steal from me the two months served in County Jail. I stood battered but tall before the desk of the head Nazi and bombed the freakish grin off his fat face with the recital of an affidavit I had composed and memorized. Having no legal training, I could only sense its validity intuitively.

My position was that Captain Churchill, a "House" official, had arrested me. I was from the instant of that arrest legally in the custody of the "House," and even in the event that Captain Churchill had somehow managed to jail me on as unlikely a place as the moon for two months, I technically would have been serving "House" time. I closed my argument with a flexing of fake muscle based on the misfortune of a "House" guard who had furnished grist for recent newspaper headlines. He was then under indictment for selling and delivering a hacksaw blade to a group of half corpses in the steel caskets down the way from mine.

So for a dramatic flexing of that personal muscle I hunched my wasted frame forward and arrogantly glued my palms to the mirror-like top of the Nazi's desk. I flinched back from a remarkable likeness of the wolfman staring up at me and switched my eyes to the fat red face before me. I told it in that low, disarming tone of voice used by sneaky cops just before they stomp or kick you into insensibility that the notorious guard under indictment had delivered, to a friend of mine on the outside, several pieces of explosive and embarrassing (for the Nazi and his City Hall bosses) mail.

His face turned from red to white to blue, and I remembered the rumors about his faulty pump. I stood there grinning and watched him choking and gasping for air. I went on to assure him that the letter contained the names of racketeering guards and an exposé of corruption within the joint that perhaps even he was not aware of. And I assured him that my friend would make public the contents of the letters if I did not get my legal release date.

I secretly hoped that convict me and my threats might have triggered a fatal attack. My emotions made of that pulse-leaping moment a monument of vengeance, an event that could not have been excelled except by the exquisite pleasure of blowing out his diseased brains. And for the first time since I'd been caged in the steel box I felt like a human being—like a man.

He seemed to be strangling as I smiled at him and slipped out the door to the escort guard waiting in the corridor for me. I paced the steel box in an agony of suspense: Was the torturer dead? Then panic and despair: I couldn't survive in the box for those extra two months! Wouldn't the muscle of my bluff and my chance for a legal release date die with him?

Later that afternoon the cellhouse vibrated with the sudden thunder of profane raillery and the feet of shop cons going to their cells on the tiers above me. I tuned my ears up high, but no gleeful announcement of the head keeper's death filtered down through the bedlam of voices and epidemic farting.

He had survived and the chances were that I would escape the steel box within forty eight hours. But suddenly I was terrified at the prospect of freedom. Almost immediately I realized why. I was caught in the nightmare bind that an older pimp faces after the age of thirty-five. He is then prone to many setbacks and disasters. Any one of them can put him on his uppers and without the basic gaudy bait, like an out-of-sight car, psychedelic wardrobe, the diamonds necessary to hook and enslave a fresh stable of humping young whores.

I still owned a portion of the mind of a young whore. But my bottom or main whore of many years had delivered my car, jewelry, clothes and other vital pimp flash to an obscure but younger, fresher monster than I. The young mudkicker had written me frequently and she had regularly sent me small money orders. She had left a Montana bordello to run afoul of a spermy gambler who ruined her commercial curves and blew away my heady dreams of mountainous greenbacks by blasting a squealer into her belly.

And now her sobby letters indicated that she was petulantly waiting for me, her favorite field marshall of cunt huckstering, to liberate her from her slum pad and her unwanted motherhood.

But she didn't know I'd had the jolting insight that I had been a sucker, conned by my own velvet bullshit that the whores had bought for a generation, about the magnificence of the pimp game. She didn't know I was determined not to join that contemptible group of aging pimps I had seen through the years and pitied as they went their pathetic way with a wild dream of new glory and a big fast stable of young freak mud kickers.

Young whores give an old pimp down on his luck merciless treatment. They flirt with him, play on him, give the corrupt old dreamer hope and then viciously poke fun at him as they coldly reject him. No, I was not going back to become one of them. And I was just as determined not to become a suicidal stickup artist or other "heavy" hustler.

But how was I going to make it out there in the free world with no training except in the art of pimping? I vowed there in the box to kill myself before I became like "Dandy" Sammy. He had been a boss pimp whom I had idolized as a boy when I was getting street poisoned.

One dazzling summer afternoon in Cleveland at the peak of my pimphood I was confronted on the sidewalk outside my hotel by an old, stooped black man. He clutched a shoeshine box and he stank of the vomit encrusting his ragged shirt front. His pitch was a poem of pathos.

I declined a shine, but the seamed ruin of his face nudged a ghost inside my skull. Almost mechanically I gave him a twenty dollar bill and went past him. His face haunted me across a dozen states and cities.

Six months later I was shooting "H" in a fellow pimp's pad. An old whore got dreamy eyed and cracked about how much bread she had made for Dandy Sammy and what a helluva pimp he had been. And then suddenly I knew who the filthy old bum with the shoeshine box had been.

Now I waited in a steel box with compounded misery, Mama was dying of an incurable disease out in California, and the guilt I felt for my neglect of her through the years was crushing. Mama's friends had sent me more than enough money for the trip to California. I had promised Mama I would come to her upon my release.

I got my legal release date and stood weakly outside the joint blinking in the April sun. I was a confused, wasted shadow of myself—unsure of in what direction lay the Southside. I chose a direction and found freedom from the box so intoxicating that I walked miles before my legs got rubbery. I staggered into a greasy spoon on the Southside and gulped down a bowl of gumbo. Peeping at my gruesome reflection in the chrome napkin holder, I wondered how my cute young whore would react to a face as wrecked as mine.

I went to a barber shop on Forty-third Street and got a shave and mud massage with scalding towels galore. I relaxed beneath the searing steam and tried to piece together exit con for the girl. I had expected the barber to perform a minor miracle, but his mirror told me I looked like my own grandpaw.

I walked toward the El station in my still blurry state of mind and stupidly decided I wouldn't go to the girl's kitchenette pad and display my ruin. Perhaps I was afraid that my sick pimp brain couldn't cope with the certain temptation face to face to peddle her plush pussy. I would catch the first plane or train leaving Chicago and send her a nice creamy letter from Los Angeles.

Then it hit me! The girl's trip to employment in Montana was still within the White Slave statute of limitations. I stopped and leaned weakly against a lamp post. I realized that I would be asking for a bit in the federal joint if I split from the girl in a way to leave her hostile.

I was one of the dozen or so black pimps the F.B.I. kept constant tabs on to nail on a white slave beef. Their deadly method was to swoop down on an angry girl, usually when she was facing a jail term for prostitution, and offer her freedom if she would sign a criminal complaint against the pimp who'd left her raw and vengeful.

I'd been shipped off once to a federal pen because I'd been careless and cut a girl loose in the rough. The greatest fear a seasoned pimp has is that some salty whore he has split from will sign a paper offered by an eager F.B.I. agent stipulating she was sent across state lines to hustle.

It was early afternoon when I went through the foyer of the tenement building and spotted her at the end of the first floor hallway. She was holding the infant in her arms and laughing gaily with an ebony skeleton who was jiggling inside an orange print tent and popping her fingers to the music and lyrics of the "Madison"—a then current dance craze.

I walked to within three feet of them before my girl saw me. For a moment her tan face was a cool, indifferent blank. And then, in a series of lightning changes, it twisted with recognition from wincing shock at my ghastly ruin, to puckered-mouth pity to the fraud of neon-eyed, squealy-mouthed ecstasy. I felt violence bubbling inside my skull, but I managed a grotesque grin and took the tiny infant in my arms. I heard the skeleton giggle derisively and dance away as I lowered my mouth to the curvy lips of my one and only (and last) whore.

I felt that old hot writhing of her lips and my tongue was instantly flogged by the wet whip lashing forth with its spray of honey. I began to wonder about how tough the exit from her life could possibly be.

I followed her into the furnished dungeon and sat in a rickety rocker beside a half-open, soot-streaked window. I pretended to be fascinated by the scabrous view of the garbage strewn alley as I frantically tried to frame exit dialogue that wouldn't get me crossed into a long bit in a federal joint.

All of the countless whores I have known and those I have controlled revealed a hunger for notoriety and for punishment, psychic or physical or both. The phony glamour and cruelty of the pimp fill these needs and are the magnets that attract and hold the whore to the pimp.

Since I was aware of these things, my strategy to cop a heel smoothly from the young whore was obvious. I had to convince her of my inability to handle her affairs and to blaze again in pimp glory. I was going to ignore her freakish yen for the punishment ritual of "kiss, kick" that is the pimp's trade.

I had to come on with low voltage, square world dialogue and saccharine sweetness. I couldn't quit her because of the "white slave" threat, and I had to be certain that she quit me not in anger, but in pity.

I held the gambler's squealer and tuned out the girl's rundown on the yoyo affairs of pimps and whores we knew until twilight.

After we had eaten a soul food supper and the baby was asleep, she lay in my arms and beat me to the nitty gritty by peevishly saying, "You haven't been rapping much, and the little you've rapped sounded 'off the wall' like a chump trick. You salty 'cause I had that sucker's baby?"

I playfully spanked her behind and said, "Sweet puppy, accidents happen to a genius, so how can I be salty with you about the kid? She's beautiful. It's just going to take a little time to come to myself after what the white folks did to me in that steel box. And I'm confused like a sucker fresh from the sticks."

She said icily, "I can dig it. But what the hell about the game and are you going to keep me in this lousy pad forever? I'm the only bitch that stayed in your corner when you went to the joint. Don't forget that."

I kissed the brown skin bomb from belly button to ear lobe and said sweetly, "Baby Angel, I'm hip you're my star, but my head is really bad. I'm ashamed to tell you how bad. I don't see how my foggy head can put together a stable of girls and control it. And besides it wouldn't be right for a beautiful young girl like you to hump her heart out to get the playing front for a washed out old nigger pimp like me. And Angel, what about the poor little kid? She needs her mama all the time and you need a man with ideas or with a job. My brain is dead and I'm too sick to work. Maybe I should split the scene so some fast young stud can come in and take care of your business. It's up to you, Baby Angel, you call the shots. Like I told you, I'm dead upstairs."

She stiffened in my arms and was silent for a long moment.

Finally she raised herself on an elbow and stared into my eyes and said quietly, "For real, I can call the shots?"

I nodded and she sprang to her feet. She slipped into a kimono, went to her purse on the dresser and dashed out the door. I heard a coin clinking into the phone in the hall.

I got up and stuck my ear against the door. I heard her placing a collect long distance call to a whorehouse in northern Michigan. The sudden racket of missile warfare between a shouting couple across the hall blotted out the girl's voice.

I was sitting on the side of the lumpy bed faking my cool when she joyously pranced in and screeched out the numbing news. It was bad, way out bad for me and Mama on her death bed out in California. The establishment in Michigan would have an opening for her three-way talent at the end of the week. She went into a detailed rundown on how to feed, bathe, burp and diaper the gambler's squealer while she was away nobly flatbacking our escape from the kitchenette dungeon.

There was at the time a very deep reason or fear that overrode the obvious ones why I was not aching to help this poor frustrated mother to employment in the Michigan flesh factory. Several years before an over-confident pimp acquaintance of mine had sent his one and only whore to the Michigan spot under consideration directly that she healed from the dropping of twin boys.

I visited mama pimp at his pad and pointed out that the town was crawling with shit-talking, whore-starved young studs, and that a dizzy young hot money tree like his was certain to be chopped down by a new master under the strain of whorehouse boredom and loneliness. He sneered and went into the usual novice pimp monologue about how "tight" he had his woman and the power of his "game."

He was surprised that I wasn't aware of the trump he held in the twins to bind his girl to him forever. He was an arrogant ass, so I made no effort to "pull his coat" to the street-tested truth that while whores simpered their love and loyalty, they were really pressure-shocked robots who prayed for the pimp's destruction and often dumped babies in alleys like garbage.

Within a month the Michigan mudkicker found her new master and the naive young pimp was stuck with a brace of howling crumb crushers. But fortunately for the twins, the pimp's mother found them adorable and took them over.

And now in the funky autumn of my life I was apparently being set up for mamahood. What with the white slave thing still pulsing, it was a treacherous and explosive situation with a five-day fuse. I considered extreme strategy as I lay beside her in midnight misery.

I decided to play the role of rapidly worsening senility. "What is usually most disgustingly flawful about the senile?" I asked myself. "No control of the plumbing, of course," I answered.

I scooted back from the girl's sleeping form and shortly managed a stout stream which momentarily made of her a peninsula. But she slept on, wearing on her lovely face the last beatific (or any other) smile I was to witness. Soon, above the din of erotic rats squeaking their rodent rapture within the dungeon walls, I joined my whore madonna in pungent slumber.

Next morning she was curly-lipped furious and my slack-jaw idiocy augmented by even looser bowels had by nightfall inspired her to masterworks of creative profanity. She roughly diapered me on the greasy couch (my new bed) with a mildewed bath towel and she literally reeled away in disgust when I gurgled like a big black happy baby.

Much later I heard her tiptoe to the hall phone and repeatedly call numbers and ask for "Cat Daddy," an ancient pimp with enormous light gray eyes and a penchant for young whores. I was praying that they made a contract together because a whore almost never sends her exiting pimp to the penitentiary when her new pimp is on the scene to witness her treachery.

The next day when the girl was out with the baby I went to the corner drugstore and talked to Mama in California. We really cried more than talked, but I felt happy that she was still alive as I walked back to the dungeon. I was a hundred yards from the building when I saw the girl with the squealer in arms alight from Cat Daddy's orchid-hued spaceship. I stopped and sat down on a stoop. She stood outside the car and for a minute and a half she dipped and nodded her head toward the gesticulating silhouette inside. I suddenly felt a weird combination of joy and loss for I realized that she was giving Cat Daddy the classic "yes" response a young whore plays out for her new pimp.

I sat on the stoop for over an hour after she had gone in. When I went in she pulled me down beside her on the bed and went into her thing. She told me in a pleasant voice that she felt very sorry that my illness had forced her to get herself and the baby a sponsor. She was moving soon, like within twenty-four hours, into a groovy pad furnished by the sponsor. But she was awfully worried about me, and perhaps I would be smart to run a game for care on one of the County institutions until our luck changed.

I strangled my wild joy (and a pang of loss) behind a blank mask and mumbled, "Baby daughter, I'm going to my Mama. She knows better than anybody how to nurse me back to the pink. And Angel Dumpling, as soon as I get myself and my game together I'll write you at that bar on Forty-seventh Street and send for you and my baby girl."

Later I lay sleepless in the stifling room watching her sleeping. Her magnificent body was nude except for wisps of whorehouse costume that seemed ready to burst against the buxom stress of her honey toned curves and fat jet bush gleaming through the peach gauze.

I remembered the fast stacks of greenbacks, the icy, goose-pimpling, hot-sweet torture of that freak tongue, and the exquisite grab of that incredibly heavy-lipped cunt in the giddy beginning when her sick whore's skull was bewitched by my poisonous pimp charisma. My erection was sucker swift and rock hard, but as I started off the couch toward her, it collapsed. I suddenly realized that I had lost all power over her and therefore in her cold-blooded whore judgment I was just another customer, a chump john. I turned my face to the wall and worried until dawn about my moves and the wisdom of willfully blowing off a young freak whore with mileage galore left to hump away.

I was fully dressed, standing by the side of the bed looking down on her, when she awoke and cringed away. I smiled and flapped good-bye with my fingers like a child. Her lips mutely formed "good luck" and I went quickly away. In the cab on the way to the airport, I felt a stab of regret that I was leaving her forever back there. But then immediately the pain was gone in the great relief of my smooth exit from her and the terrible emptiness of the pimp game. And it was good to realize that no longer would I brutalize and exploit black women.

LETTER TO PAPA

May 10, 1970

Dear Papa,

I hope you are still alive and well somewhere among true friends who are warming and cheering the late winter of your life.

Mama passed away nearly ten years ago out here in Los Angeles. Oh Papa, how she suffered before she died, and how wasted and unlike the lovely black maiden who became your bride in the deep South and fled North sharing with you an impossible dream of everlasting love, bright opportunity and dignity as a human being in the Promised Land. But at the end, at least, she could be proud and happy that I had dropped the pimp life.

Papa, I am so sorry that I still hated you the last time I saw you in that liquor store in Chicago almost twenty years ago. I am haunted now by the memory of how utterly beaten and pathetic you looked with your fragile frame slumped inside your threadbare clothing as you whiningly begged the store owner for just one more half gallon of suds on credit.

Papa, I am ashamed to confess that I stood there behind you so sick with hatred I was exhilarated, thrilled at your torment. And Papa dear, I wish I could forget the God-damn stupid, cold-blooded joy I felt when you turned your face, that tortured replica of my own, toward me. My awful hurt, Papa, lies now in the bitter awareness that understanding and compassion are the only proper responses to black men, and especially fathers forced to abdicate manhood in the racist, brute crucible that is America.

Papa, you were so shocked and happy to see me that you didn't notice my smile was really a sneer as you embraced me and stained my two-hundred-dollar suit with your tears. I paid off your eighteen dollar bill and perversely bought you a case of Keeley beer which wobbled your knees as we walked the half block to your sunless furnished room in a tenement building on Calumet Avenue.

Right away you started steering the conversation toward Mama. I knew about that everlasting torch burning inside you for Mama, so to dunk you in hot emotional grease, I lied and spun a tale about how much she loved some guy and how happy and successful she was.

Papa, I tried hard to make Mama understand about you before she died. And I don't think she went to the grave still unforgiving, hating you for hurling me against the wall of that cold water flat when I was six months old and walking away from us at the height of a subzero Chicago winter.

But Papa, I swear all is forgiven for I understand now that the most hellish aspect of America's racism is that for generations it has warped and twisted legions of innately good black men, causing the vital vine of black family stability and strength to be poisoned, hacked down by the pity, fear and hatred of black children.

What is most important to me now is that you forgive me for a long-ago brutal moment when I stupidly crushed you with cruelty and hatred. I can't forget it, Papa. The F.B.I. and every roller in Chicago wanted to bust me and I had come into the street to cop a bag of dope. I got it and was on the way back to my hideout when you ran from a barber shop and saw me pass. You were screaming my name. You were happy to see me and afraid I'd get away before you could say hello. You caught me and held me tight.

And while you were making love to me, I stiff-armed you away and said, "Damn Jack, I thought you had croaked. I'm in an awful hurry. See you around."

Your voice broke when you said, "I did my part to bring you into this world. Please, don't treat me like a dog. You look prosperous, what's your line? Are you with some big white company? Are you married to some nice girl? Do I have any grandchildren, son?"

I said coldly, "Look Jack, I'm Iceberg Slim, the pimp. Ain't you proud of me? I'm the greatest nigger that ever came out of our family. I got five whores humping sparks out of their asses."

Papa, I thought you were going to have a heart attack because the barber's apron was quivering over your heart, and your face was gray with shock under the street light. But I still wasn't satisfied. I had to do you in all the way. I jerked my shirt and coat sleeves up past spike hollow and stuck my needle-scarred arm under your nose.

You recoiled and I snarled, "Goddamnit Jack, what's the matter? Shit, I shoot more scratch in that arm in a day than you make in a week. I've come a long way since you bounced my skull off that tenement wall. Jack, stick out your chest in pride. I been in two penitentiaries already. Shit Jack, I'm on my way to the third one. You ain't hip I'm important? Maybe one day I'll make you a really proud father—I'll croak a whore and make the chair."

I walked away from you to a cab. I turned and you had collapsed in the gutter crying your heart out. Forgive me Papa, please forgive me. Forgive me, Papa.

Papa, if you are still in this mortal coil I know that you, like me and millions of other black men of all ages, have gained wonderful new ball power from the courage and daring exploits of the Black Panthers in this Eden of genocide. It is tragic that too many black fathers have always lacked something their children could be proud of and remember. Surely this genuflective, lack-luster life style molded by America's harsh repression is responsible for the irrational, self-destructive contempt and hostility felt by young black militants for elderly and middle-age black men whose survival tactics—for themselves and their loved ones—seen through history's unflattering lens appear the antics of despicable Uncle Toms marinated in cowardice.

Papa, we older black men must guard against condemning and hating the young rejuvenators of our balls for despising us and blaming us for letting them be born into this hellish society—one we at least could have risked our lives to demolish. Perhaps our black heroes of revolt would be less bitter towards old niggers if they could understand that they owe their very existence as revolutionaries to all those disenchanted black men who, since slavery, have probed and challenged America's oppressive power structure. From the risks, suffering and deaths of these anonymous heroes have evolved the awesome courage and methodology of black revolt that now intimidates the masters of repression.

Papa, you have perhaps forgotten a long ago incident that I will never forget. For on that occasion and at that shining moment the jewels of your manhood coruscated in a star burst of pride and courage that was, in that ultra-repressive era and circumstance, the purest heroism.

I was a small boy and you had persuaded Mama to let me spend several days with you on Big Bill Thompson's yacht. He was the Mayor of Chicago at the time and you were the chef on the boat during a short cruise on Lake Michigan for the pleasure of ruddy-faced politicans and Capone soldiers. The sleek craft vibrated with the coarse voices of foppish, olive-complexioned men and the drunken squeals of their brassy blonde broads.

I remember I was perched on a stool in the steamy galley watching you and your two white assistants putting together an elaborate meal when Big Bill, the Mayor, hurled himself into the galley and stood on unreliable legs glaring down at you like a silver-maned bull. You ignored him, but I saw your black face harden beneath the shiny film of sweat. And my heart beat less frantically when you moved away from him.

It almost stopped when the florid monster stalked you to the range and roared, "This goddamn meal is late! Get the fucking lead out, boy!"

Your hands worked eerily in space like spastic claws, and the stark white of your eyes flashed back at me for a pounding instant. The tyrant, perhaps infuriated by the insolent irritation on your face, shoved hard against your scrawny chest. You stumbled backward and stood with mouth agape for a moment. Then your face became feral like a killer black leopard.

And then you, Papa, nigger you from a plantation outside Nashville, Tennessee, had the courage, had enough raw heroism left in your battered black balls to clench your fists and scream out to the feared Croesus of Chicago's corruption and crime, "Don't you never put your hands on me, sonuvabitch. Don't you never call me no boy. You get your big fat red ass out of my kitchen before I go plumb crazy and whale the shit outta' you."

I sat there on the stool in a trance of fear and excitement as the huge master of the power structure stood petrified in shock and stared down at you for what seemed like eons. And then suddenly he surprisingly grinned and the grin became booming ragged laughter as he strode from the galley shaking his head.

Papa, after forty years I still can't be sure of how you got away with it. Was the colossus so secure in his self-image of power and superiority over you, the powerless inferior nigger, that he could finally respond only with amused tolerance at your indignation and rage—with perhaps a bit of that permissive admiration a master feels for a tiny dog with the guts to bare its teeth when teased beyond reasonable limits?

Or perhaps, in that galley arena with no gangster lackeys or hoodlum cops around to crush your challenge, he showed craven cowardice and camouflaged his terror with hysterical laughter. Who knows Papa, but that maybe all the power-gluttonous architects of repression and racism in America have yellow neon stripes glowing on their backs as they cower behind their police and soldiers. Papa, we will never know just why the Mayor of Chicago kissed your black ass in that galley long ago. But what ever the reason, your glorious act of manhood cannot be diminished, for you flung your challenge into the unknown and maniacal winds of a hurricane.

Papa, this is one of the few letters I have ever written in my life and it is certainly the longest. Writing it has given me more pleasure and satisfaction than any other I have ever written.

Please write me at 8060 Melrose Avenue in Los Angeles, and I will send for you to come and stay for a week, a month or forever. Papa, we need you and love you and you will be as welcome in our home as Malcolm X would be.

Sincerely your son,

Bob Jr.

RAPPING ABOUT THE PIMP GAME

In the spring of 1970 in Los Angeles, I was having a sandwich at an open-air stand when a slender black guy with a doll face and a raging ambition to pimp swooped down on me from a new crimson Buick Electra, containing the most beautiful young brown skin girl I'd seen in a decade.

He draped himself too casually on the bench across the table from me. He had the same eager, familiar look in his eyes as dozens of young black guys have had as they set out to pick and probe for the criminal treasures they believe are buried inside my skull.

Trying to stiff-arm him away from the poison before he reached for it, I said: "You've got a freak machine there. What've you done, made foreman at the aircraft plant and decided to settle down with that brown skin vision?"

A pained look came over his face, as if I had clumsily ripped the lace of his lavender see-through shirt. He snorted and leaned back arrogantly and cracked, "Ice! You ain't heard? I cut loose from that gig. I'm macking and that vision is humping for me. I'm gonna split to the track in the big fast Windy in a few days and I want you to run down the joints where I can cut into the boss pimps and get hip to where my girl can get action."

I said, "So you've just turned out and you think you're the greatest. You couldn't be more than nineteen or twenty. What makes you think you're qualified to make it on the fast track in Chicago?"

He looked away and exchanged clenched fist salutes with a trio of young guys passing in a burnt-orange spaceship. He leaned towards me and said, "I memorized the bible you wrote on the whore game, and I'm so pretty the whores cream their panties when I come on the scene. I'll have every nigger in Chicago scared that pretty Eli is gonna steal his whore. All the ones I can't steal, I'll shake down gorilla-style. And Ice, I can run a bitch up the wall with my boss dick. I know the game, Ice. I'm qualified. I'm ready for the Windy."

I sat there silently for a long moment looking at his smooth, unlined face and remembered how my own youth was lost and poisoned long ago in the dope-soaked Chicago underworld. I had seen scores of young black dudes with more guts, gab and looks than this boastful guy owned who had been mangled on the fast track.

I fought back the disgust and anger I felt; this young guy had all his life, had everything going for him to make it outside the lousy underworld. Now he was wild to chump off his life. I decided to blast his ass off and maybe, at least, turn him away from the fast track.

I said, "Young brother, you come from a nice family and I like you, so I'm going to tell you like it is. There are young pimps in the Windy twenty times faster and smarter than you who can't score for grits and greens, and they're so good-looking their asses would make you a Sunday face.

"You read and memorized *Pimp*, the story of my life, and you didn't get your coat pulled that pimping is for dudes who are suckers for jail cells and smack dealers? You think pimping is a beauty contest? You think you can fuck? There are johns, tricks in the streets that can lay your whore and suck her cunt so good she'll have convulsions with diarrhea! You take that cream puff young broad to the city and in six weeks some slicker will pump her rotten with H, and you'll be flat-ass busted waiting for your folks to send you the fare back home. I wouldn't even lay a two-bit bet you won't wind up a puddle of shit and blood in some alley."

I rose from the table and left him with his mouth ajar. He didn't split to the fast track because I run into him now and then and he always turns his eyes away. An acquaintance of his told me a young Italian customer stole the brown skin vision from the dude and he went back to the aircraft gig. I like to believe that my tongue-lashing had some part in maybe saving the young black for something more rewarding than pimping.

For several years I've been answering questions about the pimp life on TV, on radio, in the street and at teen posts. I'm going to rap about the street and the pimp for a while, and maybe answer some questions that you have posed in your mind.

The career pimp lives by a rigid code of self-discipline which projects (for his admiring whores) an image of icy composure in the face of the constant stresses, and threats of the turf. He keeps his cool despite the most voluptuous sexual temptations within his stable or in the streets.

He's a gutter god who has put his emotions and sex drive into a kind of commercial cold storage. He never gets sweeter than the amount of a particular whore's money. The codes, the rules, the attitudes of pimping are passed along to new young pimps who, if imaginative, will discover something new and cunning to add to the pimp book.

An amusing example of how the book gets thicker and slicker is that inventive young Eastern pimps are at present instructing their street whores to immediately request that new customers who approach them expose their genitals. This screening gimmick must give undercover vice cops a helluva headache, since it is against the law to expose one's genitals in public.

Many people ask if I have any thoughts about why I and others become pimps.

In the late forties, a headshrinker in the Federal penitentiary at Leavenworth, Kansas, told me that I had possibly become a pimp because of savage and unconscious hatred for Mama, who was the perfect loving mother except for that one mistake when she fell in love with a snake and tore me away from my stepfather—my only and beloved father image.

Maybe his analysis of why I became a pimp was accurate. Looking back, I remember that the most efficient and brutal pimps I have known had mothers who were drunkards, dope fiends, or whores. Several of the cruelest pimps that come to mind were abandoned as infants. One was put in a trash bin and another was stuffed into a garbage can. I am positive that as much as anything else my boyhood admiration for the flash and dazzle of well-heeled pimps cruising the poverty-mauled slums in gaudy cars inspired me to pimp.

Ego keeps many pimps from knowing the real reasons why the prostitute needs the pimp. The practical reasons are that the whore needs the pimp to protect her, to advise her, and to keep her out of jail. For another no less urgent reason, she needs the pimp to drive her, to punish her, to make her suffer so that painful guilt for her bitch dog existence can be relieved.

After all, whores are not born. Before they are "turned out," they are kick-outs from broken homes, students, waitresses, entertainers, barflies, middle-class kooks, and even daughters of preachers. But all have some conscience and know of society's contempt and loathing for the hooker.

I also discovered that whores need and use the flashy front, notoriety and phony glamor of pimps to get a sense of personal importance and worth. I don't think I ever got a dime from a whore because of any sexual prowess I possessed.

I am often asked, where does a pimp go to recruit girls for his stable, and how is a contract drawn up with a girl?

A career pimp literally is working every waking moment, sounding out potential whores for his stable everywhere he goes. A pimp's next whore could be the young bosomy girl working the elevator or desk at his hotel, she could be a waitress or a barmaid, a lush and susceptible stenographer in an office where he might legitimately visit and notice her commercial curves.

Then a pimp's next woman might be a seasoned whore that he cops in the street or in one of the early morning feeding and drinking joints catering to hustlers. And maybe a pimp's next package will be a whore from his best pimp pal's stable. Whores are like quicksilver and twice as hard to hold.

How a contract is drawn up depends on

the speed of the scene, and the individual pimp and the strength of his game. In the Southern and Western cities of the country, many pimps have a loose, jivey, unstated type thing with whores.

In Chicago and New York and other big Eastern cities, most pimps have a concrete contract situation with whores and spell out in great detail their rules and regulations and play the whores into commitment to an air-tight mouth agreement which is enforced by the threat of mayhem or great bodily harm or, in the case of a true gorilla pimp, death.

What makes young guys itch to pimp is the popular belief that a pimp's life is dream stuff, like gangs of sexy girls and money and night-clubbing. But trauma for trauma, a pimp's life is perhaps the worst type of life anybody could live. He is feared, hated, despised and walks a greased wire with the penitentiary on one side and his death on the other from other pimps, his victims, or their parents or relatives. He is constantly faced with the triple-crosses of whore-hungry fellow pimps who want to take what he has.

Any one of dozens of intra-stable calamities can occur and the pimp will blow whoreless and penniless. Then he will glut himself with alcohol or drugs to escape the painful reality of his booby-trapped life. Worst of all, when his youth is gone whores won't give him a cigarette. A pimp lives his life with a stick of dynamite stuck in his rectum. When on the hunt a pimp must spot weakness, a girl's softness to the pimp and the fast life. His personality must be like his clothes and jewelry—flashy, bold and fascinating. If he also has a handsome face and is young enough so that sleek muscles still writhe under his skin like a tiger's, he is going to have instant and pulse-leaping impact on a large percentage of the females he faces. The quality and quantity of response from a particular prospect will depend upon her background, her set of values and the state of her love life.

I can't say how other pimps spot weakness in a girl. I usually was able to spot the weakest ones by a glance held a fraction of an instant too long and of course the excitement in their eyes was obvious. I have always believed that anything I could touch I could get. I would maneuver myself into rap range and watch arteries in the temple and throat pulsating wildly, tipping me off that the girl would probably go for a cop or a "turnout." This type would also stutter under pressure and would follow me like a little dog to my pad and a contract.

In others not so clearly weak I would use powerful funky pimp dialogue to test for signs of weakness. Another type of jazzy prospect will hide her weakness behind a cool front of indifference, even hostility.

A seasoned pimp, however, will know from the texture and possibly outrageous degree of such a response whether it is real or fake.

Once I visited a pimp pal fresh from the penitentiary and a newly acquired young package of his reacted with glaring hostility from the instant she saw me.

I remember I winked at her pimp and cracked, "Baby Sis, how come meeting me put rocks in your jaws? Am I maybe the spitting double for some gorilla that kept his foot in your ass?"

She didn't answer. She poked out her jib and fled the hotel suite. I peeped at her hole card at that first meeting and I knew I could steal her, but I didn't because she was the only whore he had and I liked him.

Six months later he lost her and I stalked her and bought a wino a jug to trap her in a restaurant booth and to loudly accuse her of picking his pocket the night before. I came in just as he was frothing at the mouth and waving a switchblade through the air, and she was hypnotized with fear. I moved in and rescued her and got the contract an hour later while riding in my convertible and smoking "gangster."

I have often said pimping is like the watchmaker's art. To outsiders it may look easy, but it's tough. One of the iron clad truths of the pimp game is that, "the easier the cop, the quicker the blow."

When a pimp meets a girl with a curvy body and a weak mind and she is not a whore he must turn her out. This can be difficult when a girl has strong moral inhibitions against selling her body.

The "turn out" is an art within an art. However, I'll try to give you a feeling as to how it is done.

Pimps have an exciting aura of wicked bravado and raw sexiness that would threaten even the morality of a nun in long exposure. A girl with strong inhibitions but who has been weakened and stricken by the pimp's poisonous personality will have her inhibitions brain-washed away by the pimp.

After all, sexual inhibitions are usually formed in an early parental and social learning process which in a way is benign brainwashing, pointing up the superiority and "good" of tight sexual habits over the "bad" and loose sexual habits. The pimp in teaching the inhibited young girl to "unlearn" will point up the moral hypocrisy and greedy materialism rampant in the so-called square world. He will constantly portray socialites and actresses who marry older men as merely glorified prostitutes who have bartered their bodies for money.

In cases where a girl's inhibitions stand firm to this approach, and to his corrupting aura, the pimp will probably dump the package. But if she really has great commercial potential, he will try to trick her into her first whore transaction through the use of a prearranged con skit or mini-psychodrama.

There are dozens of these, but one of the most used and effective in my own pimp days was to have an older pimp buddy pose as an eccentric and wealthy square. He would take the prospect and me out on the town with lots of the bubbly. Then after we had partied and he had ingratiated himself to her with a nice gift and lots of smooth flattery, he would stop by my place for one last drink.

Tipsily, he would pretend he had something on his mind but was afraid to give voice to his desires for fear of offending me, his best friend and her, the most beautiful and sweetest and most understanding young lady he had ever met.

Finally, after a convincing game of hem and haw and my almost tearful pleas for him to reveal his secret desires because the girl was no neurotic prude, but a sophisticated person with an open mind, he would blurt out that he would give her one hundred dollars and die happy if he could see her fabulous body unadorned.

I would wink at her and say that I didn't believe it and that I was sure she would call his bluff. He would take out a check book, but I with high humor would say, "Oh, no you don't. This whole affair is beginning to take on a theatrical tone, and if she's going to be a star, she needs an agent to protect her interest. Give her the C note in cash."

He would peel it from a large roll and I would nod and wink as she took it and say, "It's not queer, is it?"

She would bring it to me and I'd look at it and put it in my pocket and say, "Go on, baby, strip and let our old rich friend die happy."

She would, and as she stood before him, he would jump about in excitement and exclaim, "Good gravy, I've never seen anything that came close to this. I can't stand it! I hope you folks don't get mad and throw me out of here for what I'm gonna say, but I'm gonna have to suck those luscious tits, and I'll pay a C note a tit."

I'd pour another round of bubbly, wink my eye at her and crack, "Man, she's beautiful all right, but aren't you drunk? You've been very nice to us tonight and we are your friends. Are you sure you want to give my star two more C notes?"

And so it would go with the bubbly and the C notes and the fake eccentric square would con the girl into the bedroom to turn her first trick.

The "turnout" hinges on one clear-cut sexual act for pay that, whether performed in awareness or in trickery, forces the instant and sharp emotional and moral transformation from square to whore.

Pimps with an air-tight game demand all the money a girl makes and consider it a grave offense for a girl to hold out or spend any money without permission.

That is the difference between a whore and a call girl.

Call girls usually are fragile, chicken-hearted kittens who like to spend a lot of time and money on themselves and usually like to dole out a fraction of their earnings to gigolo-type jokers who know their place and stay in it. Whores are for pimps who want all the money and full control of the woman. And whores have lots of heart and pure disdain for gigolo types.

Only rarely does a pimp ever keep all of his women in quarters where he lives, and then only if the house is big enough to afford him complete privacy. Of course, some pimps with slight class will shack up with a bunch of bitches in a cracker box kitchenette.

Also, a pimp doesn't keep track of six, seven or eight women. He can't, and he doesn't try unless he's a lunatic. What he does is play as tight a game as he can and he lets the earnings of each girl tell the story of what each girl's value is, and whether she's lolly-gagging instead of working, or really in the pimp's corner.

He doesn't try to keep a stable of whores happy, either. He can't even keep himself happy. What he does is keep them conned, confused, bamboozled and fascinated so that they will continue to hump his pockets fat with green backs. Life for a whore if she's got a pimp is around-the-clock pressure, terror and constant fear of the death-traps in the street.

Years ago, a pimp was a pimp, but now a lot of so-called pimps have a girl or two and sell everything except tours of their sphincter muscles. Many pimps are not ethical among themselves, with their women, or with people in the square world. They will only take an ethical position for a future advantage or because not to be ethical in a certain instance would cause a loss of public face or embarrassment. They are only ethical with any group or individual when it is strategic to be so.

Most pimps chump off their money. They blow it on drugs, clothes, jewelry, cars and in chrome and leather cesspools.

If prostitution were legalized only in houses of prostitution the ranks of pimps would be drastically cut. The street whore's clientele would patronize the safer, protected houses, forcing her off the streets or into a house as an employee where many older whores would decide they didn't need a pimp.

If legalized in the street the pimp would be in heaven because then one of his major recruitment problems would be gone and his girls could work with complete abandon. But

I don't believe there will ever be country-wide legalization of prostitution in America.

Perhaps you have wondered what happens to pimps and prostitutes when they get old. Do they retire and live happily ever after when the sporting life bubble bursts?

A scant few of the older career pimps I have known survive to old age. Drugs, whiskey, shootings, stabbings and the debauchery of the fast life usually doom them to a coffin in early middle age.

The survivors become bar owners, bums, bookmakers, slum hustlers, stick men or flunkeys in sneak gambling joints. A few marry well-fixed business women or widows. Others are raving lunatics in mental hospitals. Several became preachers of the gospel.

Whores who survive the murderous ravages of the sporting life square up and become housewives and mothers. Others become madams, thieves, pimping lesbians, business women and religious fanatics. As to whether any of the survivors I have known are living happily ever after, I can only say that the squared up ones I have run into through the years claimed they were glad to be out of the life.

I have squared up and cut all underworld cronies loose. My few acquaintances, and the couple of friends I have are about evenly black and white, and include writers, a theatrical manager, an actor, home makers and just ordinary nine to five people.

For many years I used drugs and drank hard liquor. I don't use anything now. I don't even smoke cigarettes any more.

People are always asking me what my thoughts are now that I have squared up when I see whores and pimps doing their thing in the street.

What they are really asking is, am I envious and do I miss the pimp life? I see pimps and their girls working the streets and remember how it was to crack the whip and to count the fast green. But before I can start missing the old days or wanting to play the game again, I always remember the tension, fear and grief that no pimp can escape. I feel no envy for pimps—only pity that they waste their youth and intellect.

Last summer a young lady in a television studio asked one of the most important questions I have ever been asked: "Do you expect any problems, emotional or otherwise, with your children when they get old enough to know their father is a notorious ex-pimp and ex-con?"

I have given the matter a lot of thought

and I don't think my lurid past will create any major problems for any one in my family. I am confident that my children's intelligence will permit them to cope with any poison the haters might throw at them.

They will be further insulated against twisted accounts of my past life after they have read my autobiography—*Pimp, the Story of my Life*. In fact it might enhance their love and respect for their old man to discover how he clawed and crawled up out of the stinking sewer of the underworld in this racist society to give them life and love. And how incredibly Old Daddy now smells something like a rose.

BABY SIS

She wasn't any kind of star when I first met her back in Chicago in the mid-fifties. She was just a big-eyed skinny kid singing funky blues with a shabby black revue. After the last show, a fellow pimp persuaded me to go backstage to rap a bit and maybe cop a couple of the cute young broads of the chorus for stardom in the street. A pair of cuties had been eye-balling and grinning down on Pretty Bert and me all during the show. But still, I wasn't red hot to shoot at a show broad. In my book they were spotlight freaks who weren't worth a pimp's headache to "turn out."

The kid singer was in a corner of the ratty dressing room rapping with the two packages we had eyes for. I caught a flash of nappy crotch behind a ragged curtain where a guy was dressing. Pretty Bert and I moved into the scene and started quizzing and sounding. We found out the revue had played its last night in Chicago and the members of the show were waiting for their road manager to bring news of the next booking—and their wages for two weeks work. The owner of the theater finally came to say he wanted to lock up and go home. And he told the fifteen uptight entertainers that he had given the road manager the show's bread at the beginning of the last performance. On the sidewalk somebody put in a call to the road manager's hotel, and was told he had checked out.

We went into a greasy spoon down the street with the stranded troupe. Bert and I sat in a booth with the target broads and the kid singer who was a pal of the broad I was stalking. We sensed a kill, so we ordered plates of soul food for the hungry girls and listened to them crying the blues while waiting for the food. The two dancers did all the griping. Holly, I'll call the kid singer, sat silently staring with those unforgettable big sad eyes out at the midnight street people infesting the intersection at 63rd and Cottage Grove Avenue. Just before the food came, she burst into tears and fled to the washroom.

Holly's pal rushed after her, and the other dancer told us that Holly was only sixteen years old. She had left home two months before hoping to make enough money so she and her arthritic mama could get away from a horny step-father who was frantic to get in Holly's panties. Holly's mama couldn't work. She had left her youth and health in cotton fields down South.

After the girls had eaten, Pretty Bert moved his game ahead and split with his package to play on her. My game was a bit handicapped because my package was tied to the juvenile Holly. But there was something real, warm and likable about the big-eyed kid that maybe touched my deeply buried streak of sympathetic sucker. She instantly liked and trusted me. She called me Big Bro and I called her Baby Sis.

So instead of figuring angles to cut Holly loose from my prospect in the rough, I took them to pick up their things from a slum hotel room they were sharing. I took them to my pad and put Holly up in an extra bedroom. The dancer and I sat down in my freaked off lavender and gold living room for serious rapping. Right away the beautiful broad cracked she was hip to what I was and she wanted to try me, and the fast scene, because she was tired of dancing. So I just reached into my skull and unfolded the contract.

Early next morning I went to work on the Holly problem. First, I made her call her mother who happened to be very sick. But Holly got the good news that the crazy stepfather was off the scene. Holly broke down and wept like the homesick child she really was. That afternoon I drove her to the airport. When her flight home was announced, she embraced me and kissed me and said, "Big Bro, I won't ever forget what you have done for me. I'm going to pay you back some day." Naturally I didn't hip her that I bought her ticket home with bread her pal had humped for with a Chinese chump that very morning. I hugged her and said, "Forget it, Baby Sis. You don't owe me anything." She walked away toward the gate. I said, "Good luck, Baby, and I hope you score for some nice young stud back home and raise a big happy family."

She braked sharply and spun around. She came back quickly with short, explosive steps. She looked up at me with enormous brown eyes aglow and said in her draggy big-foot country voice, "Big Bro, I'm going home to look after Mama, and nothing else. When I get eighteen, I'm going back on the road, and someday I'm going to be a real big star, a rich boss star. Bye-bye now, and don't forget I told you so." I watched her unglamorous frame move through the gate. I walked to the car and wondered where in ego hell a skinny black girl who sang funky blues with a so-so voice figured to become a star in a world loaded with high voltage broads who had a bitch of a time scoring for the daily grits and greens.

Holly's pal humped and gave me her bread for a year before she hit the wind and re-entered show biz with a cute little tap dancing dude with a face just like Bambi's, the cartoon deer. I didn't go into shock. I hadn't figured to hold a show biz broad for more than two months anyway. During that year she and Holly kept in touch by mail and phone. Holly was working in a laundry and singing a gig now and then. At least a dozen times I got on the line briefly to rap a few words of encouragement and affection to Holly, but I lost contact with her after I blew her pal. Several years of lightning-paced street struggle might have wiped Holly and her pal from memory: I said might have because Pretty

Bert, who amazingly still held the dancer he had copped from the black revue, was a show biz buff. He read *Variety* and followed the entertainment news in black and white magazines and newspapers and passed along to me modest items about Holly and my ex-mudkicker. When Holly first surfaced she was singing ballads in not-so-swank eastern cabarets and attending acting school. Then later she sang, danced, and acted in several off-Broadway musicals and plays.

Pretty Bert had a five-whore stable, but he was the most discontented pimp I knew. He'd read an item about some black female theatrical star getting thousands a week for her act and bemoan the fact that a brilliant and gorgeous dude like himself was pimping his heart out on a gang of stinking street whores instead of taking off long bread from a glamorous black performer. He spent a lot of his time stalking his dream prey in a bar on East Sixty-first Street run by an ex-boxer. The joint was a watering and feeding spot for many of America's top black sports and theatrical stars. And there were leggy cutie-pie vultures and cold-blooded toothy hustlers staked out in the plush murk to ambush celebrity bankrolls.

Like I told you, Pretty Bert stalked street

whores only part time. I stalked them full time so I wasn't on scene with Bert at his favorite bar when Holly, my play Baby Sis, blew in from New York with troubles again. It was a snowy night in December around midnight and I was busily building breathtaking air castles for a dazzled new package when tipsy Bert called and said a fabulous young bitch was standing by to say hello. Her voice was ragged with tension as she blurted out her problem and begged me to come to the bar. I told her to have Bert bring her to my place. She said Bert had just gone out the front door with a broad and her problem, who was in the men's room, would stick his knife in her if he caught her slipping out of the bar. Suddenly she slammed down the receiver.

Her problem was a cruel ex-gorilla street pimp who had turned idea man and pimp manager for black female performers. I had known him back in Detroit many years before as the kind of pimp who had to spill a whore's blood before she could quit him. Other pimps shunned him as a suspected police informer. Holly had fled his terror and beatings, but true to the gorilla code he had followed her to Chicago and threatened to kill her before he'd let her quit him. He had moved her and her trunks from her loop hotel suite into a southside hotel around the corner from Bert's favorite bar. She hadn't called in the cops because she was afraid of notoriety. Holly wanted me to talk to the gorilla, do something to get herself and her trunks cut loose so she could open in two days at a fancy club on the near Northside in at least fair mental condition. After that engagement she was going to the West Coast.

It was against code to butt into the affairs of a stud and his broad unless the broad was a whore and I knew she wanted me for her new boss. But I decided to case the trouble scene and try to help Baby Sis without heavy melodrama like killing—or worse, dying! Since the gorilla knew me and was in my home town I figured I could con him or bluff him out of Holly's life. I made three calls before I located a ferocious-looking hustler who could do a cop bit that gave suckers diarrhea. I had done time with him at Leavenworth and we were tight. I gave him the rundown and he promised he and a partner would be on the scene to back my play on the gorilla.

I dropped a .25 automatic in my overcoat pocket and drove the mile or so to the bar. Holly was alone in a booth clutching a glass and staring at the table top. She glanced up and saw me coming toward her. She came out to the aisle and hugged me. Her once scrawny frame was all softness and curves, and she looked like an African princess, with her hair worn in a then uncommon Natural. We sat down and she said in a shaky voice, "Big Bro, what am I going to do? He's been snorting H all day and he's so crazy I'm afraid to be alone with him."

I said, "Where is he now?"

She glanced fearfully toward the front window and said, "I think he's across the street in a peddler's car. He's not far away, and he told me that if he had to he was going to drag me out of here when he got back."

I said, "Sit here with me until he shows and then go along with everything I rap to him."

Holly and I were seated side by side in the rear of the room facing the front door. I was next to the aisle with my overcoat folded across my knees in such a way that I could dart my hand in for the rod in case the gorilla got a sudden urge to do surgery.

He came through the front door and except for a few lines around his tight mouth he looked like the same dapper little snake

I'd known in Detroit. He stopped and stared at us with dope-glazed eyes for a moment. He came past the crowded bar to our booth and teetered on his heels as we stared into each other's eyes until Holly mumbled, "This is Ice."

He shifted his eyes and said coldly, "I know him. Now let's get out of here."

I felt Holly tremble. I said firmly, "She's not going anywhere, brother. You blew her to me. She's my woman and I'm gonna go by the book. Now sit down and have a taste and let's work this thing out like players."

The guy went rigid and his handsome yellow face twisted ugly. Just like he hadn't heard a word, he said harshly, "Come out of that booth, bitch." He stepped back and stuck his right hand in his overcoat pocket.

I saw my two fake cops standing near the door watching us. Beneath the table top I started to ease the rod from my overcoat pocket. The weight of it didn't feel right. A probing finger told me why. In my haste I had forgotten to shove a clip of bullets into the automatic! I was younger then, and quicker, and I was sure I could disarm a pint-sized knifer wobbly with a skull-load of H.

I was dumber then too. I said stoutly,

"Clown, this is my woman, and I'm gonna look out for her if I have to go to the chair."

He sneered, and as his hand started out of his overcoat pocket, I started to rise and wind my overcoat around my left arm to fend off stabs and slashes. I fell back into the booth and froze. The guy was holding a snub-nosed .38 close to his body so people at the bar and in the booth ahead wouldn't wake up to the drama. He leaned over and put his left palm on the table top like he had stopped by for a bit of chit chat. He leveled the wicked snout of the .38 at my heart and almost whispered, "Motherfucker, I should make you suck my dick. You ain't going to the chair. I'm sending you to the morgue if you don't get out of my bitch's face and stay out. Now slide out slow and let the front door hit you in the ass."

He stepped back and I went past him down the aisle toward the front door. The fake rollers looked puzzled and went through the front door ahead of me. As I passed them on the sidewalk, I said, "Heater in his benny's right raise. Bust and bull scare him for a couple of hours."

I went to my car up the street and in less than five minutes the gorilla walked out of the bar with Holly and was seized front and rear by the burly grifters and hustled into their car. I drove down the street and picked up Holly. Within an hour and a half a truck had moved Holly's trunks to my place. At four a.m. my man the grifter called to report that the gorilla had been bull scared into taking a train back to New York.

I began telling him how much I appreciated the favor, and how I had a piece of bread he and his pal could pick up, when he cut me off. "Forget it—wait 'til I'm pressed. We squeezed more than two grand in jewelry and cash out of him."

I was reading in bed when Holly came to my bedroom door and asked for a cigarette. I lit one for her and she sat on the side of the bed smoking it. Her nude body gleamed like curvy sable through her gauzy pink wrapper. But I felt nothing. She fiddled with an embroidered rose on the bedspread and said softly, "Why did you do that for me tonight?" It was a tough question then, and even now I'm not sure I know the real deep down answer.

I said, "I never liked that nigger and I hated his style. And you are my play Baby Sis. You're safe now. Count your blessings, and forget the whole thing."

She stood up, smiled and said carefully, "I

can't forget it. You don't understand how I feel." She waved her hands helplessly about her head and went on, "I want to do something. Do you mind if I lie down with you?"

I laughed and said, "I've never had anything but whores in this bed. Baby Sis, you can't qualify for this bed. You want to be a star and you won't 'turn out' for me. I gotta pimp for my bread, and I can't do casual fucking with no understanding. Besides, I'm not the kind of slob that could lay his Baby Sis. Now get your beautiful square ass out of here. I'm expecting my bottom woman any minute."

She giggled and leaped into bed with me and kissed me a dozen times on my face and neck. She was leaving the room when I said seriously, "Holly, if you must do something for me, stay real like you are if the white folks make a star out of you on the West Coast. Don't become a phony black caucasian star."

She walked back to the side of the bed and said earnestly, "Slim, I'm always going to be real. I won't let anything change me. I'll never be a phony. I'll stay black inside as well as outside. I love being black."

Holly got rave notices at the Northside spot, and three weeks later she left for the

West Coast. A companion made the trip with her. He was a handsome young piano player who lived across the hall from me. I liked Al, and Holly flipped silly for him. Holly called me when she got to the coast, and for a year and a half she and Al kept in touch. She was making a living, but nothing spectacular had happened for her when I got busted and started that tough bit in the steel casket in 1960. I lost touch with her.

I was living in L.A. in the late sixties when Holly's career exploded star dust. Now I don't mean she had the luster and impact of say young white stars like Ann-Margret, or Joey Heatherton, or even of black Diahann Carroll. But she was getting roles in movies and important guest shots on TV and it was rumored that a wealthy older white guy had his nose wide open for her and was sponsoring her lavish life-style and a palatial house in the hills. According to the standards of black America and the black press, she was like at least a dozen other black female performers in America considered a star. I made no effort to contact her until I ran into Al, the piano player, at a party at John Wesley's pad. He was a black actor who had played a role in the movie "Up Tight."

I asked Al about Holly, and he came on

with heat. He said, "Ice, I had to split. The girl is sick in the head. She's a freak for white studs and she tries to think, act and talk like a white broad. All of her so-called friends are white. She's a pure Oreo. You know, like the cookie, black outside and white inside. She's ruined and she's got a headshrinker. Find out for yourself. I'll give you her number, but believe me, she'll make you puke."

Few if any visibly black people have not secretly hated themselves and wished to escape the misery of a black skin. But Al had accused Holly of going beyond the wishing to live the delusion that she had escaped the trap of blackness and had become an adored equal in a racist white world that considered her deniggerized and no longer tainted by the black world with its struggle and rage.

A week after I talked to Al, curiosity made me dial Holly's number. A maid or somebody took my name and a moment later Holly came on the wire with a gush of high gloss vivacity and unreal excitement that I had called. She demanded in her weird, new sleeky-accented voice that I rush right up to the hills to see her. I agreed to visit her the next afternoon.

The next day a uniformed white broad with thick ankles led me through Holly's luxurious house to a kidney-shaped swimming pool at the rear of the house. Holly squealed in apparent joy at the sight of me and came out of the water glistening in the sun, and beautiful in a gold bikini. Her only flaw showed in the deep shadows beneath her eyes—and she came weaving toward me as if she had been drinking heavily.

She planted a damp kiss on my cheek and we sat down at a poolside table. She removed a bathing cap and a golden blonde wig fell to her shoulders. We sat there making smalltalk and sipping drinks from a portable bar beside the table.

Then I got slightly personal. I said, "Baby Sis, level with me. Are you really happy and satisfied now that you've made it?"

She frowned and her mouth tightened. Then she showed her snowy capped teeth and said merrily, "How could I be anything but happy surrounded by lovely things and beautiful people? Don't I look happy?"

"I guess you would, to somebody who hadn't known you when," I said. I leaned toward her and took her hands in mine, I looked into her eyes and said gently, "Baby Sis, you've changed, and our people are losing respect for you. They are saying you despise your blackness. You don't want that, do you? Is it true what they're saying? Level with me, Baby Sis."

She jerked her hands away and stood up. Her eyes were blazing. Her face looked old and hard framed by the silky caucasian blonde wig. She was furious and drunk. She spat, "All right, here it is, and don't call me Baby Sis. Say *your* people, your niggers, not mine. Niggers didn't put me up here. White people did. I don't give a goddamn about niggers, or what they think about me. There are scads of important beautiful white people who have forgotten I'm black. I don't need niggers, and when I was suffering and scuffling down there with them, not one nigger in my whole life ever did anything for me. White people are in my corner. They love me, and that's where it's at."

I got to my feet while she was still raving, and stood looking at her until she stopped to catch her breath. I said, "Holly, I risked my life in Chicago to help you, remember? And I happen to be a nigger."

Her jaw hinge dropped and she turned gray. I turned and walked through her house to my car in the driveway. As I drove off I looked back at her house and remembered the flash of nappy crotch in the ratty dressing room where I first met her. And I remembered the skinny kid singer's gratitude at the airport in Chicago when I sent her home to her mama, and her boast that she was going to be a star.

She had become a star all right, a black caucasian star.

A GODDESS REVISITED

I am convinced that most pimps require the secretly buried fuel of Mother hatred to stoke their fiery vendetta of cruelty and merciless exploitation against whores primarily and ultimately all women.

Throughout most of my life my unconscious hatred for my mother leapt painfully from the depths like bitter bile from the guts of a poison victim. But I believe that the unfeeling rejection of me by a lovely young girl at an emotionally crucial period of my life might well have been another reason why I became a pimp.

Her memory, her face, her voice haunted my lonely nights in four penitentiaries. For me she was a Goddess and perhaps such an elusive, unearthly, wonderful creature, real or imagined, torments the private dreams of every man. I will never forget the flavor of those days long ago when the Goddess and I were in the spring of our youth. Somehow the bittersweet mystique of the northwest corner at Third and Galena Streets in Milwaukee, Wisconsin, will always have a wistful charm and sorrow for me. For it was there in rain, shine or storm that I sped early mornings to glimpse, to hear the melodic voice of the Goddess before the bus arrived to whisk her to Catholic Messmer Junior High. I wasn't welcome to visit the Goddess at home. You see, her Creole mother didn't approve of me. I was too black.

It was in the spring of '33, I think, that I met the Goddess. Hilarious jokes were making the rounds, like: "That wasn't no girl you saw me with last night, that was my brother." Anyway, it was just a short time before that fabulous cripple charmed himself into the most exclusive club there ever was.

Mama was on earth then. I remember how attractive and regal she was. Once a month Mama and I would pass that corner. I'd stare at it and feel little firecrackers of excitement popping off inside me.

We'd be on our way to a gigantic barn-like building. Mama would always proudly square her shoulders before we stepped inside. The slippery sawdust on the rough pine floor would be like shredded ice against the slick, stiff soles of my county relief brogans. There was a fresh pungency in the melded odors of prunes, onions and potatoes stacked inside chicken-wire cubicles.

Tattered paupers filed past the cubicles. Anemic joy lit their drawn faces as bored county clerks shoved a month's ration of relief groceries across the dusty cubicle counters. They would eagerly fill their gunny sacks and shuffle away to the street with their treasures.

When our turn came, Mama would hold her chin high in the manner of a queen accepting gifts from her subjects. You can't imagine how my skinny six foot frame would tremble when I'd hoist our sacks to my back. I remember how the coarse burlap would sear my palms as I stumbled to the sidewalk.

Mama always brought a twenty-five cent piece with her. There were bootleg taxis about the building. The hustlers would be waiting in flivvers to haul people with gunny sacks home.

Many times Mama saved the quarter. A good guy called Giggling George would be out there on the hustle. He and Mama had been kids together down in Nashville, Tennessee. He'd take us home, and the only time he'd stop giggling was when Mama would try to give him the quarter fee. He'd get real serious and act like Mama had insulted him when he turned it down.

One Christmas, George gave me an exciting gift. It was an old .22 rifle. He had cleaned it and polished the walnut stock to a rich patina. I enjoyed blasting out the brains of the hunchback rats nesting in our cellar. Sure old George drank too much. It's true he had that ugly giggle, and yes he cursed a lot. But he was the kindest guy that ever was.

Oh yes, after I met the Goddess, I'd often have a crazy wish that Phillippa (that was her name) and her mother would be standing in that charity line for groceries. I guess I thought at least we could have had hunger in common. It never happened.

Her mother was a beautiful widow, a coldly arrogant octoroon. She was color sensitive too, acting like a half-white house nigger in slavery times who was suddenly made boss of the whole damn plantation. Cordelia Cordray was her name, and she was to blame for that corner at Third and Galena in Milwaukee, Wisconsin, being the most poignant corner there ever was.

Now, I'm not so sure about the year that I met the Goddess. But I'm damn sure of the day of the week. It had to be on a Sunday morning. Two slightly uncommon events had occurred the night before. Mama and I lived in a flat over Steve's Bar, at Eighth and Galena Streets.

A curvy push-over called Three-way Rosie lived up at Tenth and Galena. Her old man was an ex-heavyweight fighter who ran a sneak poker game in his home every Saturday night.

Rosie had given me this time slot in her very busy schedule. We were on the grass in her back yard. I was fiddling with one of her buttons and looking up at the Big Dipper in the brilliant sky. Strange thing about her was, one of her buttons was a dud. Every Saturday night I'd fritter away crucial time. I'd forget which button lit her fire. Finally Rosie flamed, and moaning she started working me out the straight way.

Suddenly a shower of kitchen light rained down on our mad thrashing. Rosie's old man stood glaring down at us. It was lucky for me that I was sneaker shod. I yowled and leaped straight up out of the squishy valley like a black tom cat from the top of a red hot stove. I slipped through his clutching hands like a buttered eel. He didn't have even a remote chance of catching me. I vaulted the back yard fence and torpedoed down the alley. I heard his angry bellowing and the pounding of his feet die in the sultry spring air.

That was the first event that makes me certain I met the Goddess on a Sunday morning. The second event happened less than an hour after the first.

Recreation has its valid place. Unless you're a yard-wide square, you need a bit of excitement now and then. Except for the chase scene, the grass game with Rosie was pure recreation.

In small towns a guy has to search out his excitement in the most common ways and places. Perhaps I was hopelessly jaded, but I could never get goose pimples watching the neighborhood mechanic tune up a car motor. Watching the sky for shooting stars gave me no celestial bang. And I would even completely ignore a bustling construction site.

Believe it or not, I got a charge watching mock murders. I guess you have to be black and live in a ghetto to be able to understand and appreciate that kind of thing. But look into it some time when you have nothing else to do.

On a Saturday night, I'd spend hours at

my upstairs window. I'd watch old drinking buddies horse around down on the sidewalk in front of Steve's Bar. Even though it was almost always drunken play, it was still exciting to see their knives and pistols flashing under the street lamp.

I guess it was so exciting because at first I couldn't ever be sure that it wasn't for real. Let me tell you, when those savage pranksters bared their teeth and rolled their eyes in fake madness it was hard to tell. Often one of the phony victims would flop around on the sidewalk like a dying chicken.

The night before the morning I met the Goddess, I saw Giggling George on the sidewalk. His best friend, Slick Shorty, was standing looking up at George.

Shorty had his back to me screaming up at George, "George, gimme mah dime you owe me. I saw you bust that half a buck across the bar. Gimme mah dime, George. Ah don' wanta croak you. Gimme mah dime, George."

George exploded, "Man, you ain't only slick, you crazy too. You been paid that lousy dime with interest when you guzzled my bottle of gin dry. Now get outta my face, little nigger. This is Saturday night, and I ain't for wasting it waiting around county hospital for them doctors to take my foot outta your ass."

George turned his back on Shorty and lumbered toward his jalopy at the curb. He was giggling up a storm. Then I saw Shorty slip a gleaming butcher knife from his waist band. Even when Shorty bear-hugged George from behind, I couldn't be sure it wasn't just another mock murder. Poor George screamed like a sledge-hammered calf in a slaughter house. The butcher knife in Shorty's hand was blood streaked when he leaped back from George. I heard a dull clatter when Shorty hurled the blade into the gutter and sprinted away.

George spun around facing my window. He stood there looking down at his ragged belly. His guts gleamed in the glow of the street lamp like ropes of crimson pearls. He tore his phosphorescent eyes away and tried to pump his leaden legs to flee the oozing horror at his waist. His legs buckled and twisted and entwined like magnetized pretzels as he slammed to the sidewalk on his back.

I rushed down the stairs to the sidewalk, where a small, silent crowd stood looking down at him. I looked at his face. His eyes were bucked wide and his fat black lips were moving. I stooped down close to him.

Through a gout of blood he burbled in a child's plaintive voice, "Bobby, ain't it a low down dirty shame? Shorty done kilt me."

His eyes closed. He heaved a heavy, liquid sigh and lay still. I cried there on the sidewalk beside him until I heard the squeal of a police siren. It was the real thing that time. George was a good guy. I really liked him. I went to bed, but I didn't sleep. I couldn't get butchered George out of my mind.

Now you can see why I'm so sure it had to be on a Sunday morning that I met the Goddess. I heard Mama coming in around three a. m. She had served a banquet for a rich white woman. I tossed and turned, wishing for cheerful daybreak, until finally the sun slit night's treacherous throat with a golden butcher knife.

Later I heard Sunday school buffs laughing on their way to the church around the corner. I had the worst headache there ever was. I heard Mama humming a hymn, and then shortly the metallic clicking of the boiling coffee pot's lid. I got up, took a bath and went to the kitchen for a cup of coffee. Mama was at the sink washing navy beans to cook for our dinner.

She turned toward me and said, "Good morning, Mr. Red Eyes. My heavens, you look bad. Bobby, I hope you're not drinking. George Rambeau was killed last night in a drunken fight on the corner. The police have that dwarf buddy of his in jail."

I said, "Mama, I got an awful headache, but not from drinking. I saw the whole thing last night. George wasn't fighting. His pal, Shorty, executed him for a dime. Mama, do we have any aspirin?"

"No, we don't, but there's a half dollar on top of the icebox. Get some at the drug store, and you can keep what's left for pocket change. And Bobby, for God's sake don't tell anyone you saw that killing. The white folks might lock you up until after Shorty's trial. I hope he gets a life sentence. I'm going down on my knees to pray for poor George's soul."

I dressed and went to the drug store at Seventh and Walnut. I stepped inside. There she was at the soda fountain on the first stool near the window. The bright morning sun ignited tiny blue bonfires in her shimmering black hair. She was sipping a Coke. I forgot the worst headache there ever was.

I feigned an interest in the magazines on the rack beside her. My captive eyes were chained to her. I stumbled to the stool next to her. Her lilac perfume whirled my brain on a wild, fragrant, merry-go-round.

I stuttered, "Good morning."

She turned her yellow, fawn face to mine. Jade jewels coruscated in her huge, green, almond-shaped eyes. There was a dazzling slash of faultless ivory in her face when she gypsy violined, "Good morning."

Everything was a blur until I had walked her home. I came out of the trance on the steps of Roosevelt Junior High School at Eighth and Walnut. I was deliriously aware of a powerful post-hypnotic suggestion that the Goddess had said I could call on her that evening at eight o'clock. I just sat there on the steps hallucinating her voice, her odor, her face until late afternoon.

I got home at five o'clock. Mama was frantic. She thought I had flapped my jaws and gotten jugged as a material witness hostage.

The navy beans were done. But I wasn't the least bit hungry. I took another bath and spent the next two and a half hours shining my brogans, finger nails, teeth and hair. I ironed a razor crease into my Sunday corduroys.

Mama was awed. She asked, "Whose party you going to?"

I said, "Mama dear, I'm in love. I have a date at eight with Phillippa Cordray."

Mama frowned and shook her head. "Yes, I've heard about her and her mother. They're big shots from New York. They came to town a couple of weeks ago. But isn't she out of your league? Mrs. Williams told me they're high class and they have a beautiful stone house. Her mother teaches in an all-white school. I've heard she's passing for white. Bobby, please don't get hurt. I'm afraid you're too brown and we're too poor."

I was a love-stricken fool playing against a stacked deck. Mama's plea didn't register until too much later. But never since has spring been so magical, so memorable. I floated through the lavender twilight to the Goddess. As Mama had told me, she lived in a gray stone house on Fifth Street. I rang the door bell. My mouth was dry and my palms were gluey with sweat. Small wonder. How many times in a guy's lifetime does he call on a Goddess?

She opened the door and smiled at me. She said hello and her voice was perfumed smoke tinted with moonlight. She wore a flowing lime chiffon dress. In the lavender glow, she looked like a nymph who had fled Botticelli's *Allegory of Spring*. I just stood there mutely with my fifteen-year-old heart savagely mauling my rib cage.

She took my hand and I followed her into a dazzling gold and white living room. Cordelia Cordray, an older, harder version of the Goddess, stood near an alabaster grand piano with languid feline grace eyeing me from head to toe. Almost imperceptibly she seemed to wince at my harsh clothing. She delayed an icy, taut second before acknowledging my introduction with a mute dip of her spectacularly coiffed head. Then she flounced from the room with a hostile look on her face.

Hurt? Sure I was, but in the presence of the Goddess I soon forgot the bitch Cordelia. I was having one miracle of a time just gazing at the Goddess and hearing that moonlit voice describing the wondrous excitement of New York City when Cordelia made a trilling sound and the Goddess excused herself and went into the dining room and through a swinging door to the kitchen.

I sat there on the sofa listening to the velvet bellowing of Gabriel Heater, a newscaster, and hearing the jagged tone of a quarrel coming faintly from behind the kitchen door.

Curiously, I pressed my ear against it and heard Cordelia say, "Sugar Bunny, how can you say something like that about me? We are not in the military. I did not and I will not ever command you to do anything. I am suggesting that you are wrong to encourage and clutter up my living room with that unkempt little alley creature when he is so patently not your type. Be patient, Bunny, and select your boy friends from the professional group in town."

There was a long pause before the Goddess said angrily, "Baloney, Mother, he's clean and neat and he has good manners. What's really wrong with him?"

Cordelia said evenly, "Alright, Sugar Bunny, you asked for it. He is completely wrong for you from those county gun boats on his feet to his nappy head. His parents, aside from being paupers, are probably drunkards, thieves, ex-convicts or you name it. And he is so wretchedly black my flesh crawls at the remote possibility that you would be insane enough to let him violate you, not to mention the threat and disgrace of a nigger-type grandchild."

I didn't wait to hear more. I slunk from the house, vibrating in a hot straitjacket of humiliation and rage. I was a half block away trying desperately to figure an angle to murder Cordelia without leaving clues when

I sensed scented smoke rising anxiously behind me. I looked over my shoulder and stopped.

The Goddess' hair was flying in the purple light like an indigo banner as she ran toward me calling my name. "You heard! You heard! I'm so sorry. Please forgive us!" she sobbed as she squeezed my hands and pressed the dizzying softness of herself against me.

But all the excitement as we embraced was inside my head and riotous chest. She walked to Lapham Park with me and we sat on the stone steps of Roosevelt Junior High planning how, because of Cordelia, we would take our friendship underground.

I walked her back home, nearly. I blurted out I loved her and then I recited the words of a touching poem by a poet whose name and most of whose words I have now forgotten. But it went something like, "Darling, I feel so sad and strange that all those years before, could be before we met. Don't you wish there had never been any other lips, any other sweethearts? Darling, don't you wish we could blot them out just as the smoke from a cigarette rises and fades into nothingness?"

I summoned the courage to brush her

cheek with my lips and bashfully turned and sprinted away.

Our secret underground points of rendezvous were at the drug store soda fountain where we first met, Lapham Park, the balcony of the Miller movie house downtown and especially every school morning at that enchanted place, the northwest corner of Third and Galena Streets.

The spring, summer, and fall of that unforgettable year of the Goddess went swiftly. It was in the first week of December that the cream of the giddy dream started to sour. I had hauled my lovesick young square-ass out of a downtown jewelry store, where on layaway reposed a gleaming gold compact afire with simulated rubies and diamonds. The price was an astronomical forty dollars, and I had been buying it for six months with a shine box in the streets at five cents a shine. But what the hell, how often in a lifetime does a guy sweetheart around with a Goddess?

I was walking toward the Miller movie house when I saw the Goddess come to the sidewalk clinging amorously to the arm of a tall, curly-haired, half-white guy and get into a shiny Model A Ford. They kissed deeply, long and hard before speeding away.

I leaned weakly against a lamp post with my mouth open. I knew the guy's father was a big shot with a coveted steady position as chief technician of toilet brushes and mops at City Hall. The Goddess had told me that the young guy was adored by Cordelia and I knew he had been calling on the Goddess at home for several months. But the Goddess had assured me that she really had no interest in him at all.

I had understood. It was like the guy was a cover so Cordelia wouldn't get wise that the Goddess and I were sweethearting around. She had lied to me, and I had the biggest headache there ever was as I staggered home.

Everything was lies, quarrels and hurt after that, and on Christmas Eve we met for the last time as children at the drug store. Christ! She was so beautiful and innocent-looking in her hooded white wool coat and scarlet boots. I just sat there gazing at her like a simpleton for a long time.

She sat silently sipping a cup of Boston coffee. Finally, I reached into the pocket of my tattered lumber jacket and withdrew the jeweled compact and gently placed it in her lap and wished her a Merry Christmas. She frowned and hefted the gold-foiled package in a delicate palm.

She slipped it back into my pocket and said softly, "It feels awfully expensive. You really shouldn't have. I can't take it."

I said idiotically, "You gotta take it. I ain't got nobody else to give it to."

She shook her head and said firmly, "I am so sorry. Try not to hate me and please forgive me, but I have to get married."

I was speechless with shock and despair. She stood up misty eyed and squeezed my hands.

I choked out, "But you ain't got to do nothing like that."

Her bottom lip trembled and without sound her lips said, "I'm pregnant."

I jumped from the stool and seized her arms and shouted, "You can't be! I've never done it to you!"

She burst into tears and pulled herself free and ran into the night. I'll never forget that Christmas Eve, how in my juvenile pedestal reverence for the Goddess I sat there long after she had gone, unable to cope with the fact that the curly-haired guy had indeed fucked my sacrosanct Goddess. And how in my agony I babbled my sorrow and hatred for her and every girl I'd ever known and ever would know.

I sat on the stool until the owner tapped me on the shoulder at closing time. The next several months were a horror of excruciating Goddess withdrawal agony. One spring day, when she was eight months gone, I saw her walking into a store with Curly Top. She was so bloated, disfigured and deformed that I ran home and wept in the attic for hours.

That night I felt myself encased in rage and fury so poisonous that I went searching for him with the ancient .22 rifle that Giggling George had given me. Finally I spotted his car outside Cordelia's house. I crept to the side of it and saw him playing the grand piano with his head thrown back in song. I put the back of his head in the rifle sights and was squeezing the trigger when for some reason I glanced away at the Goddess. She was seated on the sofa looking at him so worshipfully and with so much helplessly pure love that I lowered the gun and left.

A broken neck, a cracked skull can heal and so also can a broken heart, I discovered. I got my first penitentiary bit about two years after that Christmas Eve in the drug store. I got out and did another bit in the state of Wisconsin before I got wise and left town.

I had an obsession to be a pimp. I became one, and a hard and brutal one at that. But curiously, vivid memories of the Goddess could always be evoked by the faintest trace of scented smoke in some woman's voice or perhaps sunlight exploding blue light in a mane of jet hair.

Twenty-five years passed and I was on the highway to Milwaukee for a visit. I got there at night and went to several homes and bars to shuck and jive with acquaintances and old buddies I hadn't seen in a generation. I didn't ask about her at all. Toward daybreak I found myself at the bar in an after-hours spot owned by a guy I had grown up with.

It was crowded and dim. I was talking to a broad who had lived next door to me in our kid days when I glanced in the back bar mirror and saw an elderly gray-haired woman with a deeply seamed yellow face filching a bill from the shirt pocket of a drunk passed out at a table behind me.

She came away and went to the end of the bar and threw a dollar bill on the counter. She stood there weaving and shouting for Old Taylor. My heart lost rhythm at the phantom flicker of moonlight in the whiskey-stained voice. I stared at her crepey, wattled throat as she flung her head back and hurled the double shot down her gullet.

She turned and went out the door and I considered the possibility that the time and whiskey-hacked old crone of seventy could be . . . But no, it just wasn't possible. After all, she could be at most forty. And besides she had been heartbreakingly beautiful, protected, cultured and with every advantage. She could never get ugly and debauched in a million years, I thought, as I tossed the whole ridiculous idea out of mind and gave my most seductive pimp wink to the bosomy young fox smiling at me down the bar.

Two hours later I was bored, nauseous with the prattle of the fox and my old home town. I slapped palms all around and stepped out into the bright morning sunshine. I passed the old crone talking to an elderly white man carrying a lunch pail. I wondered as I walked to my car if the old lady was optimistic enough to think she could find a buyer for her decomposed charms.

I was running the engine a bit before moving away when I saw the old broad moving down the sidewalk toward me. I wanted to gun away to avoid her, but there was something familiar and eerie about the rhythmic, swaying, girlish heat in the walk of such an apparently old woman.

She stuck her head through the open window and grinned a jagged Halloween pumpkin smile and cackled, "How about a lift to Walnut Street, big shot?"

I studied every wrecked plane of the yellow fright mask. I saw a faint lance of green fire in the blood-shot almond eyes, and saw how the tip of the still delicate nose tilted up and how the gray-riddled black hair still leaped away from the temples in great, curly, tumultuous waves. And because I was hurting like hell to see her like that, I had to get away from the sight of her.

I said gently, "I'm sorry, lady, but I'm not going in that direction."

She frowned and said impatiently, "Well, how about spending a fin with me for a half-and-half?"

I shook my head and said, "I'm not in the mood, lady. Why the hell don't you retire and get off the track?

She stepped back and shouted, "You black motherfucker, mind your own business. Who the fuck . . ."

I pulled away and headed for the highway. I passed the enchanted corner at Third and Galena and remembered a lovely young girl and how the sun ignited tiny blue bonfires in her hair. And I was glad I had kept my cool and not crushed her back there with my masterworks of creative pimp profanity. For even though brute life had hacked her hideous, she was still for me and always will be . . . a Goddess.

VIGNETTES:

CONQUEROR JACKSON

He was blue-black, squat and powerfully muscled, and visaged in the craggy image of a caveman. He was likable and charming enough when his luck was funky to get an extra fin from icy-hearted pawn brokers and a buck and a half of my last deuce. He should have been an entertainer, but he literally burst his heartstrings to make a career of, in his words, "taking good money from bad girls." He was regarded as a colorful joke, a sentimental clown by other pimps because Conqueror Jackson invariably fell in love with his girls, and he thought the pimp game was a fuck-in.

In fact his monicker was hung on him by contemptuous pimps because of Jackson's almost psychotic sexual delusion (perhaps shared by millions of studs in much milder degree) that he was some kind of gladiator in the sex act, capable of inflicting an unprecedented orgasmic impression on adversary cunt and vanquishing it, conquering it, enslaving it with his heroic, invincible dick.

But his greatest flaw and handicap as a pimp was a sympathy and admiration for all women; he lacked the ruthlessness and deep hatred for women that all career pimps must have. He was just too soft a guy deep inside to play the hard pimp game.

I went to his pad in Chicago to snort some cocaine when we were twenty-two. He had one young mahogany-colored three-way whore who had freaked his nose wide open. And sharing Jackson's pad was a tall, champagne-toned young pimp fresh out of the penitentiary and sleek and pretty and deadly as a coral snake. I knew the punk was rank, but Jackson was crazy about him so I stayed on the dummy.

The predictable happened, and a month later Conqueror Jackson burst into my pad at the Pershing Hotel on Cottage Grove sobbing and snotting, "That dirty motherfucker stole my girl and all my furniture and clothes."

Jackson roared, "I took that shit-colored

double crosser in and fed him and he crossed me. Hear me, Jim, it's square business. I'm gonna find that lousy nigger and run him back up his mammy's ass. I ain't gonna croak him for stealing the bitch and my stuff, but for principle, Jim, for principle."

I bombarded him with street logic and begged him to recognize the hard pimp law of "cop and blow"; somebody has to lose when somebody wins. But he wouldn't hold still and he split, spitting fire, thunder and murder. A week later he trapped the young whore-thief in a booth in a Chinese restaurant and smashed the dude's neck with his hands. Jackson did a fin in the joint for manslaughter. He got out and for a while copped the bread for his grits and greens ripping off suckers with a short con mob.

One salubrious summer afternoon I paused to watch the Conqueror toss the broads (manipulating the cards in three-card Monte) under the Forty-seventh Street El tracks for a gargantuan, young, mean-faced black guy. Jackson's cap man (confederate) heckled and persuaded the mark to blow close to a C note to Jackson with such violent enthusiasm that the mark woke up. He flexed his fortress of muscles and knocked the cap man into a coma, and demanded his lost break back from Jackson, who courageously instructed the colossus to do something relatively difficult for him to do to himself as he squared off before the foamy brute.

I moved away and from a sensible distance watched the giant monotonously deck the Conqueror with a lightning array of hooks and crosses that would have made Sugar Ray drool with envy. Then while the Conqueror was rising from a knock down, the giant cocked back a muscular leg for kick action. I saw the Conqueror's right arm lash out toward the giant's crotch and a laser lance of rippling silver light slash across the fly of tight dungarees and a sudden tiny spring of shiny crimson leap in the sunshine.

I walked over and helped the Conqueror to his feet as the whimpering giant leaned buck-eyed against an El pillar. And then my eye was attracted by something that looked like a misshapen, black, bloody marble in the dust. I looked at the glassy-eyed giant who seemed amused at the scarlet pouring from the butchered-off tip of his organ, like a little kid playing the game of "who can pee the farthest."

The giant bled to death and Conqueror did an encore at the penitentiary. The years galloped, and in '68, almost thirty years later,

I saw the Conqueror again while out for a walk in Los Angeles.

He spotted me and picked me up in a battered '58 Cadillac. He was white haired, stooped, and the flashy chorus of muscles that once danced beneath the indigo skin had vanished behind an ugly curtain of fat, but he was still talking shit.

On the way to his favorite bar he said, "Slim, I heard you come in off the street and now you pimping on paper for the writing game, and ain't nothing wrong with that, for you. I ain't got no kinda education or nothing and my ticker is fucked up. I got a light porter gig I do at the airport. But I'm a player and I'm gonna conquer some young fine fox and come back like gang busters. Hear me, Jim, cause it's square business. I gotta pimp my old ass off just once before I cash in. All I got to do is get the right young bitch in bed so I can do my thing. And that's square business."

He stopped on a side street off Western Avenue and we got out. Then he did an extremely odd thing. He unlocked the trunk of the Caddie and brought forth a long, heavy logging type chain, and several gigantic padlocks. I stood there and watched him wrap the chain around his rear bumper and then around the trunk of a palm tree. And then he secured the works with the padlocks.

On our way to the bar around the corner he chuckled and explained, "Slim, I been getting a little light weight bad break, so I figured out that angle to keep the repo bastards from copping my hog when I ain't in it."

Several months passed before I drove by the Conqueror's favorite bar and decided to drop in and jaw a bit with him. The joint was quiet and deserted except for the barkeep. I played a record and asked about the Conqueror.

The keep pursed his lips, shook his head and said sorrowfully, "Jackson dropped dead two weeks ago right down the street in the motel. They say he died riding one of those hot ass tramp fillies, young enough to be his granddaughter. I liked that old bullshit fool, everybody did. I just don't know why he'd go out and put his bad heart in a trick bag like that. Why did he have to chump off like a . . ."

I walked away to the sun bathed street and sadly remembered that sunny day long ago when I first saw him as an orphan, a grimy hobo, fresh in Chicago from Georgia aching to be somebody important, to be a big shot in the city. And for days I kept thinking, what a helluva way for him to go, what a lousy, stinking, disgraceful and ignoble death for a Conqueror.

VIGNETTES:

AN OLD WHITE SLAVE AND SHIELD

During my long, idiotic quest for something for nothing, I met under non-sociable conditions in four penitentiaries an army of hacks, bulls, screws—prison guards. At least 98% of them were fear-ridden scum trapped in a paranoia that they themselves had created through physical and mental cruelties inflicted on hapless convicts.

But one seemed different or perhaps age had withered the brute in him when I met him. He was "Old Tom," the guard on duty the night those half corpses down the way from my steel casket hacksawed themselves free into the nightmare shadows of the darkened cell house to stalk unwary "Old Tom" with that peculiar patience that men driven mad often summon.

Like I said, Tom wasn't too stinking as hacks go. He wouldn't motherfuck you if you asked for extra aspirin and he was on rare occasion almost kindly and even concerned about my health. I saw in his eyes and heard beneath his casual chitchat his awareness of and his desire to escape the trick bag of atrocity and danger that cops and screws are put into for the protection and benefit of the corrupt big wheels of the Establishment.

One night I put Tom's humanity to the stiffest test. I was desperate as hell to hit on him for a special favor before his shift ended. But I kept stalling and watching him passing my cell on his rounds of the cellhouse until I felt I would blow up with tension. I got off my bunk and stood by the cell door. At last I heard the scrape of his feet making the next-to-last round of his shift. His startled eyes glowed in his seamed face as his flashlight caught me standing in the quiet blackness. I whispered, "Tom, this telegram came from California today. My old lady is dying and I'm the low-life ass that's been pushing her along for twenty years. I wrote some things she has to hear before she goes. Will you please take the letter out with you tonight and put air mail special stamps on it? I can oil you with a double saw note. How about it? Huh?"

He grunted and flashed his torch on the telegram. I unfolded it and held it in the spotlight. He grunted again and growled, "Tough luck about your mother, but what the hell you think I am, a patsy? You goddamn well know it's a serious violation of the rules for an officer to lug a kite for an inmate. Now get the hell in that bunk and send your mail through regular channels tomorrow. And money is contraband. Haven't you got enough problems? Get rid of it."

I said, "I can't use the joint mail. With the censoring and a three cent stamp on it, she could be buried before the letter got to California. You're the only hope I got."

He looked at me for a long moment and said, "Make a deal with somebody on the day shift." I said, "The only one that would do it for me is off tomorrow." Tom shrugged and went down the tier. I paced the dark cell and wondered how long before the ass-kicking goon squad would descend on me, tear my cell apart, and hurl me naked into a freezing stripped-down cell. I wanted to bang my stupid skull against the steel bars for cracking to Tom about the double saw buck and even the letter. I was certain Old Tom was going to finger me to the goon squad before he went home. After all, every black con with savvy knew that all the white screws in the joint were snakes.

Believe me, I was sweaty sorry I had chumped off as I sat on the side of the bunk holding the wadded bill over the john. I turned my ears up high for the clanging of the cell house door as the goon squad came stomping in to visit me.

I heard the sound of Old Tom's feet on his last round so I leaped onto my cot and closed my eyes. He stopped in front of my cell and blazed his torch on my face. I fluttered my eyelids open sleepily and raised myself on an elbow. Tom growled, "Come off that act and get the hell over here with the kite."

Crazy bolts of suspicious lightning flashed through my skull as I stalled there on my elbow and tried to figure what kind of angle the old screw had in mind to cross me. Then it struck me that it had to be that Old Tom was uptight for dough, bread, and it was the double saw buck that had shoved him back to me. I got off the cot grinning and holding the letter out toward him as I walked to the cell door. His face was hard in the glow of his torch as he quickly scanned outside and inside the envelope. His torch etched impatient tiny arcs of streaky yellow light as he said, "All right, where the hell is the twenty?"

I pushed the bill through the bars. He took it and folded it lengthwise. And then he did the goddamndest flabbergasting thing for a double-crossing white snake screw. He placed the bill in the letter to Mama and ran his tongue across the flap and sealed it. I was speechless. He mumbled, "Your old lady will need it." And then he walked away into the cellhouse murk. I sat on the side of the cot for a long time in utter confusion. Yes, Old Tom had lots of humanity and his type was a rarity among the low life hacks I have known.

But to those bitter ambushers in the cellhouse blackness, Old Tom was just one of the torturers, one of the keepers who turned the key in the terrible steel boxes. When "Old Tom" passed their lair of shadows, they lunged forth ferociously. The pulpy sound of steel bar clubs against Old Tom's skull and body and his piteous child-like wailing for mercy brought my already sick skull to the very end of its slack. Tom, the Establishment slave and shield, got his retirement all right —in a wheel chair.

Cops and prison guards are, as everybody

of course understands, necessary for the protection of society's members and their property. A tragic injustice and irony lies in the fact that most of the victims of America's bestial cops and prison guards are black people, often denied due process of law and the opportunity to make a legitimate living. The irony is that the cynical clique of ruthless men who masquerade as champions of justice and humanity are really the architects of repression and murder at home and abroad. Cops and prison guards are the ruthless slaves and shields and the victims themselves of these viciously cold-blooded men who perhaps become emotional only when their power is threatened.

I know I can never forget that night the old guard suffered and bled because his masters had created a society of such hatred, torment and bigotry that men had been driven mad. The terrible irony is that Old Tom, the best of the worst, had given decades of his life to the system and to the power mongers lying back that horrible night in safety and in comfort behind Old Tom's gory shield of torn flesh and shattered skull bone.

VIGNETTES:

THE PROFESSOR

I met him by accident, which is a common aspect of calamity. I was fresh from the steel casket and huckstering insecticides at the time when he opened his apartment door with a tolerantly unctuous "Ph. D. in psychology" smile. I looked over his shoulder while pitching to him at the glamorous disarray of his writer's workshop. He had no bugs, so my pitch was in vain, but before I turned away I asked him if he were indeed a writer. He was, and he invited me in to a coke and a chair, for which my weary dogs were grateful.

In the course of our chat he asked if I had ever written anything. I dashed downstairs to my ancient jalopy and came back with a short piece (inspired by a true situation) about a black pimp who discovers that one of his girls has testified against him to a secret grand jury. He lures her to the countryside and punches her senseless before he douses her with gasoline. He stupidly strikes the one match left in a cover advertising a bar he owns, and after hurling the match to torch her off, he tosses the cover away and is on his way to the chair in record time.

The Professor wasn't visibly awe-stricken by the work. But when I revealed (by an account of several street vignettes) that I had been a pimp for a generation on an especially fast track, his excitement yanked him up and down in his chair like a black, hook-nosed yoyo.

He got the obsession to write my life story and during the next several weeks I recounted on his tape recorder the material to be used in the projected "pimp" book. I grew to like him and to admire his superior intellectual gifts and writing experience. There were many things about him that showed he was dangerously flawed; like he lived his life as much as possible among white people and in white prestige bistros like the Polo Lounge. And for a professor of psychology, he had some unique hangups, like the cute, intelligent black girl that spent her every free moment in his bed. He admitted he loved it, but was ashamed to be seen with her in public.

One day after a long session of taping he leaned back in his chair and said softly, "Well old buddy, I am going to start transcribing the material from the tape for a first drafting of preliminary chapters. I want to be fair with you in the financial aspect of our book, so what do you think is a fair shake? Maybe we can think now about a tentative seventy-thirty arrangement."

As I have indicated, I liked and admired the guy and I was a newly born babe in the so-called square world, so I honestly figured the guy was unselfishly offering me the seventy percent and wanting thirty percent for himself.

I grinned like a mark and said, "The hell with that kind of split, pal. We're friends and we go fifty-fifty right down the line and don't you worry, you won't have to write the book by yourself. I'm going to write a lot of it myself."

The guy literally winced away from my remarks with a sudden grayish pallor suffusing his face and in a kind of strange chokey voice said, "Yes, perhaps that is fair, but you can trust me to write the book."

We talked for an hour after his near heart

attack, but he wasn't really there if you get what I mean. When I got ready to go his eyes found the configuration of the fake Persian carpet utterly fascinating.

He said hesitantly, "Don't get the wrong impression. I know we can trust an oral agreement and each other all the way, but maybe the best of friends should put business agreements in writing. I can have my lawyer draw up the proper papers. You want to think about it for a few days?"

I thought quickly, in a contract drawn up by this bird and his lawyer, I can get tipped off fast whether he is my friend or a thieving nigger motherfucker.

I said sweetly, "What the hell, pal, let's get the ball rolling. I'd sign now if the contract were ready."

Three days later in Beverly Hills we went through plush lavender and redwood catacombs to the inner sanctum of a florid-faced wheeler dealer in a four-hundred-dollar suit who was oozing distractive charm like a pickpocket whore in a creep joint.

I read the proffered document twice before I caught it. The criminal who had constructed that contract was a master swindler to make the likes of a Yellow Kid Weil seem like a congenital idiot by comparison.

The goddamn thing was eerie in its burglarious perfection. The fifty-fifty split, all of it was there. But one clause of only several words nullified the whole document and raped my rights. As I said before, I was just free of the steel casket and I was a very edgy citizen, so my first impulse was to slay them both with bullets in the head from a .25 automatic (carried because the Professor was suspect as an enemy) dangling from a length of elastic inside my right coat sleeve.

But I stood up and smiled broadly and said, "Gentlemen, I would like to take this home and study it for a day or so. May I?"

On the drive back to my jalopy, the Professor was very quiet and I had a helluva time keeping my cool. Several days later after an agony of worry and indecision, I went to his pad and told him that I was aware of the crooked contract. He pleaded his ignorance of its sucker clause and begged me to forget the whole affair and suggested we go with just an oral agreement.

I rejected his proposal and his friendship, and because I had once really liked the guy, I told him to go fuck himself in the coolest, kindest voice I could muster.

That evening I sat down and started writing a fifty-page outline of what was to be *Pimp: the Story of My Life* by Iceberg Slim.

After my disappointment and bitterness over the Professor's attempt to run the game on me had died, I rummaged through my mind and found the reason why I had reacted like an emotional con victim when I got hip that the Professor's dogs were clay. After all, I was a former street creature who had survived in a jungle of cunning and treachery for like eons. I suspected that the real reason why was bigger and deeper than either the Professor himself, our fouled-up deal, or the fact that I had liked the guy and resented his violation of my trust. In the past I had been crossed by underworld friends and been grimly amused, not stricken.

I remember when I was a boy the great respect, admiration and envy my pals and other members of the black masses had felt for educated, successful members of the black middle class. They arrested every eye as they cruised their class A autos through the streets wearing their fine clothes and the well-fed, pampered look of the affluent. They were stainless, inspiring symbols to many naive, low caste blacks aching to live a bit of the elusive "good life" before the grave.

When I reached my early teens one of the

most respected men in the black community, a lawyer, was convicted of bilking an invalid black woman of her life savings. Everybody was shocked beyond description, for the lawyer had been a Mason and a deacon in the church. He had had the whole shining black middle-class facade.

But years went by, and now the awakened black masses have nothing but contempt and hostility for the black elite who victimize poor blacks with shoddy goods, crooked services and sky high rents for fire trap flats.

And perhaps worst of all with political betrayal. Most middle class blacks are honest and interested in the uplifting of less fortunate black people. But many of the so-called black elite, foolishly driven to ape the extravagant life style of wealthy whites, must swindle and racketeer to keep their phony images.

The reason I reacted to the Professor's clay feet the way I did was because in a way I had been reborn into the square world, and I wanted him to be a model of class and principle like the envied, respected black men of my early boyhood. Now, in the Seventies, a grim question arises: Will the contempt and disdain that many middle class blacks feel for lower caste blacks increase and deepen the distrust and hostility that the black masses feel for their privileged brothers? Will Black Revolution first shed the blood of black middle-class predators in the ghetto?

VIGNETTES:

THE BLACK PANTHERS

A day or so after December 8, 1969, when a small band of Black Panther super warriors defended the main office of the Southern California Chapter at 4115 South Central Avenue in Los Angeles for an incredible five hours against a frustrated Los Angeles Police Department blitzkreig, I visited Panther headquarters, or what was left of it.

Unfortunately much of black opinion about the Panthers (their newspaper and community benefit programs notwithstanding) is shaped by the news and writings of white columnists that appear in the white press, and also by what appears in the so-called black press (often controlled and/or secretly owned by whites) relative to Panthers.

Through rhetorical sleight-of-hand, the white press and its columnists have produced, except for rare posturings of fairness in reportage of police-Panther confrontation, the fraudulent illusion that cops are heroic victims and Panthers criminals whom the cops must imprison or destroy to protect us all from their homicidal compulsions.

The black press had (until the December 8 blitzkreig) for the most part reinforced the grotesque illusion for blacks by reporting almost verbatim what the white press had printed. I do not recall ever reading an in-depth interview with a Black Panther in the black press.

In the wake of the monumental blunder by the Los Angeles Police Department in its invasion of the black community, black civic leaders and the black press leaped into the fray (with unprecedented, sulphuric rhetoric) to protest the high-handed tactics of the raid, and to weather eye justice for the Panthers.

But the printed and jaw-bone flak issued by so-called "good niggers," who had remained silent when Panthers and other black people were being beaten, shot and killed in the streets by police, seemed only to express outrage that their trusted white power structure confidants had let them suffer humiliating surprise when the spectacular police raid came off. And too, for the "good niggers" there was ominous portent both in the brute surprise and in the raid's deadly extravagance, for the "good nigger" realized that in the final analysis a nigger is a nigger is a nigger, and that his genuflective ass has no immunity from threat, terror and death.

I reached the 4100 block on Central Avenue around noon. Police cars were cruising past the war-ravaged facade of Panther headquarters. Through the open door I saw dark figures feverishly working with the debris of battle.

Although I had not suffered anything close to a massive brainwashing relative to the Panther image, my mental portrait of them had in the typical and widespread fashion of the older, hip and unhip black man been painted with a secretly envious and prejudiced brush. Because all sane old niggers who tell the truth, including myself, had been scared shitless of police in their youth. So, as I approached the office entrance reeking of eye-stinging tear gas fumes, the Panther image in my brain was of a young, courageous but jivey, kooky, dude who stayed high, talked incessant shit and exuded immorality.

Several youngsters in the casual uniform of the Panthers came from the office to the sidewalk just as I reached the entrance. Their eyes streamed tears from the residual gas inside. I approached a muscular fellow who seemed to be the leader.

I said, "I'm Iceberg Slim," and stuck my hand out, palm up.

He looked at me and hesitated for a long moment before he smiled thinly and slapped his palm against mine.

He told me his name and said, "What's happening?"

I answered carefully, "Man, I had to come down here to say that as an older black stud I admired and appreciated the way you showed America your balls the other day in that police . . ."

I didn't finish the sentence because one of the other young Panthers standing nearby overheard my remark and cut in. "What did you say, man? You mean pigs, right?"

I nodded my head. The leader said, "Cool it, this is Iceberg."

The others moved in around us. As I stood there chatting about the raid and my writings, I had the sobering realization that unlike the hundreds of non-Panther black youngsters who had recognized me on the street and admired me as a kind of folk hero, because of my lurid and sensational pimp background, the Panther youngsters were blind to my negative glamour and, in fact, expressed a polite disdain for my former profession and its phony flash of big cars, jewelry and clothes. Their only obsession seemed to be the freedom of black people.

I noticed a thin, light-complexioned, secretary-type Panther, with a sheaf of paper under his arm, silently scrutinizing me.

He stepped forward abruptly and with curly-lipped contempt said, "Nigger, you kicked black women in the ass for bread. How many you got now?"

I was stunned, instantly furious, and my first impulse was to chop him down with still-remembered masterworks of pimp profanity. But I responded with love and understanding. Is there any other response for an old nigger surrounded by Black Panthers? I alibied that when I was young there were no reasonably dependable and available sources of big money and a sense of importance for a slum kid except as a hoodlum dope peddler or pimp.

He wouldn't accept it and attacked my suspected criminal moral attitude with renewed ferocity. As I stood there absorbing the violent tongue thrashing, my anger evaporated and I was given an insight usually denied a black man my age.

The realization that these young black brothers were the antithesis of the distorted image carried in the collective mind of America's older, brainwashed blacks moved me dramatically. I stood there joyfully aware of the fact that Black Panthers are the authentic champions and heroes of the black race, and are as a whole categorically superior to that older generation of physical cowards of which I am a part.

I mumbled goodbye and moved through a gathering crowd of sightseers. I was grateful for the acrid presence of tear gas fumes swirling about the sidewalk which gave a non-sentimental cover for the rare and genuine tears rolling down my joyous old nigger cheeks.

MELVIN X

It happened on one of those hostile late summer mornings in L.A. in 1970. The hoodlum smog, having terrorized the sun into hiding, now hurled stinging stilettoes into my eyeballs as I approached the entrance of the Black Students Alliance office. I walked into a dim cavern that seemed haunted by some fiery spirit, a feeling heightened by several poster images on the lumpy walls of Melvin X, the assassinated revolutionary.

A reddish-tan young dude rose behind a counter at the murky rear of the room and stood motionless. I felt that something more than a length of pine flooring separated my generation from that of the wary young man facing me. I strode to the counter and bellied against it in a relaxed way. Sticking out my hand I said casually, "I'm Iceberg."

The wiry body lost none of its tension and the light eyes twinkled coldly with amused skepticism. "You are?" he replied.

On the counter I laid a book bearing my likeness on its cover. His eyes zoomed from the paper image to my face in a double check. Relaxing, he told me his name and his hand came forward to meet mine.

"I came here to say how sorry I am about the loss of Melvin X and to get an intimate picture of what he was like in real life. I have a new book in the works and I'd like to be able to rap about Melvin X in it."

The slim young man said softly, "What do you want to know about Melvin?"

"Were you close to him? Do you have any idea how his last day was spent? Just rap and I'll take notes."

He heaved a sigh and began talking. "Melvin had a way about him, a power that drew all the brothers and sisters close to him."

"Can you run it down?" I cut in. "You know, like what feeling did Melvin's power arouse in you and why? Did you fear him? Did you and the others perhaps . . ."

Suddenly the man's palm was wagging in my face to cut me off as his other hand yanked at the bill of his gray cap. In the careful manner of an impatient school master speaking to a retarded student, he said, "Man, are you for real? Nobody feared Melvin except the enemies of freedom and justice for the people. Respect. Powerful respect. That's what we felt for Melvin, because he was real and there was absolutely no bullshit about him. He worked and lived only to help the brothers inside the torture chamber prisons and to educate and serve the people outside in slavery for the struggle for freedom."

He caught his breath and leaned toward me, light eyes ablaze, and said with evangelical heat, "The people loved Melvin because they knew Melvin was prepared to die for them and the struggle. Melvin's power was in his integrity and the beautiful respect and trust thing between him and the people."

Gently I asked, "Did you see him on that day? Before he was . . ."

A spasm jerked at the corner of his mouth to cut me off. His teeth gnawed at his bottom lip before he nodded. I felt the tremors of powerful emotions. His eyes softened and glanced past me at the open door. His face, unforgettable in the pale light, seemed ancient and haggard yet at the same time boyishly fresh; a face both savagely hard and softly innocent. In that sorcerous instant I realized our kinship, for his face was Melvin X's, mine, all black people's. It was a living flesh and bone montage of the ancestral nobility, beauty, bravery, misery, pain and struggle of our black race.

Finally the young man said softly, "Yes, I saw Melvin come through that door for the last time on June 6th. It was in the afternoon. I don't know why but somehow Melvin always looked very tall coming through that doorway. He was actually only five nine or ten. I guess he always looked taller because of the beautiful way he had gotten himself together inside."

"I picture Melvin as being strict," I said. "You know, tough on any brother of the BSA that he caught goofing off. Was he?"

"Melvin was so respected that he never had to stay in a real tough bag. He would come through that door and, you know, Melvin never just came on a scene—he exploded on it. The brothers sitting along the walls would stop rapping and look up at him. Sometimes Melvin would notice that the office needed straightening up or something. Then he'd look around at all the faces with those piercing brown eyes of his and chew the brothers out. But they respected and loved him and dug that he was right to stop bullshit when there was work to be done. They dug his concern and love for them beneath the hardness."

"Did he ever confront any of the phonies in the black middle class?"

The young dude smiled wryly before answering. "Melvin often appeared at meetings of those game-running black bourgeoisie and his mere presence intimidated them. They knew he was aware that their Oreo noses were rammed up Mr. Charlie's ass. And they probably suspected that for Melvin, the cream, the real elite in Black America were the masses imprisoned in funky ghettos."

I listened to a great deal more about Melvin X before I walked back out into the casket-gray morning. For days after I talked to many others who had been and still were his followers.

Melvin X was the kind of effective revolutionary perhaps most feared by the enemies of freedom and justice. He had not risen to revolutionary stardom with its clutter of hounding TV cameras, hatchetmen news reporters and, in their wake, the blood-thirsty sharks of law enforcement. The energies of the revolutionary star are sapped by constantly defending himself from killer cops and from a long penitentiary sentence or even execution for a trumped-up capital crime.

Melvin X had not been hobbled by notoriety. He was a mere 22 years old, a student at UCLA and the father of twin one-year-old sons at the time of his death. But his followers told me that he had already developed great revolutionary savvy. He moved quietly and powerfully among the street niggers whom he loved so much—educating them, gadflying them for the precious struggle.

Melvin X was an intellectual who had the rare gift of relating to all mental levels from pompous egghead to grade-school dropouts. He was respected for his iron integrity, his consistency, and the courage and rage that moved him to say such things as:

"We have prayed too long, we have meditated too long, we have talked too long without acting enough. We were never brought to America peacefully and as long as America remains it must never be allowed to forget the blood and suffering of our mothers, the humiliation and degradation of our fathers and the ruination of our children.

"If all the black people in America is the

cost that must be paid in order to insure future generations to come of a better world, then fuck it. If we have to kill every man, woman and child who stands in our way, then fuck it. If we have to destroy the world in order that the universe will not be polluted, then fuck it. We will not allow ourselves the luxury of life at the expense of freedom. . . . It is by the gun that we have been enslaved and it is only by the gun that we will be liberated.

"America is nothing more than a war criminal who has to answer for the most atrocious acts that the world has ever experienced. America will be executed and instead of a funeral there will be a victory dance, instead of a tear, there will be a smile and instead of pain there will be joy. Our Africa, our God, our children, our spirits will all be called upon to destroy you, America. We shall not fail. We have accepted violence as a way of life and death as an inevitable end."

Melvin X said much more that made him an object of admiration and love for his followers and of fear and hatred for his powerful enemies. I don't believe that Melvin X the realist expected to survive to old age, and I'd bet a C note against a nickel that he faced the assassin's gun with icy "kiss my black ass" courage and bitter regret that, unarmed, he would be taking the trip into darkness alone.

As his body was being lowered into his grave at Compton Cemetery, a barrage of gunfire could be heard crackling from a nearby pistol range. A sorrowful black brother with eyes brimming tears said softly, "Ain't it a bitch? They practicing to kill black people. Them pigs ain't hip they playing boss funeral music for Melvin."

One sweltering dawn shortly after Melvin's funeral I took a walk. As I walked miles through the sleeping black ghetto, I saw an amazing sight, a phenomenon. Gigantic spray-painted and chalk-drawn legends had blossomed on countless concrete walls and building fronts. They were grim bouquets of rage and sorrow to the memory of slain Melvin: Avenge Melvin X! Kill the pigs! Remember Melvin X! Resist to exist! Off a pig! Seize the time! Revolution is for trying! Pigs are for dying! Remember Melvin X!

I walked for hours and everywhere I saw the angry legends. Suddenly there was a freight train rumble of thunder. The morning belonged to Melvin X. I found it easy to imagine that standing a trillion feet tall, he was somewhere way up there in the bleak, gray heavens with his head cocked to one side, exhorting his street niggers in the voice of the thunder and with his brutally coded love and tenderness, to hurry the revolution and make the enemies of freedom shit blood.

America is being led to her death by racist power junkies coasting on a stupid trip—the fatal fantasy that soldiers and police can crush and destroy with clubs and guns an indestructible force: the hunger of the human soul for dignity, justice and freedom. And the American public is gobbling up the con that the emerging holocaust be stifled with gasoline.

The spiritual and physical victims, the enraged black and white wretches of this racist society, are multiplying and thriving like deadly plants in the rains of repression. Must the livid guts of America and its cops be bombed out and splattered on the wind before the deaf and blind power hypes stop their suicidal tripping and recognize the doomsday rage of the Melvin X's, hear and honor their just demands for dignity, justice, freedom?

RACISM AND THE BLACK REVOLUTION

From what Mama told me about him, I know that Thomas Jefferson Jones was six and a half feet of black satin sex stimulant. His presence flicked on wicked lights in the eyes of black females for miles around. White women, when white men were about, turned eyes away from the ebony Adonis moving with the glamorous grace of a tiger through the small Southern town on some errand for his boss, the owner of the cotton gin.

Mama, if my memory serves me true, first told me about him when I was seven years old, and repeated the story countless other times through the years until I left home.

I remember the lyrical way Mama described him and how soft and slumberous her eyes became whenever she talked about him and how sad she became and the funny way her voice shook when she told me about Jefferson Jones' last night on earth, when a pack of sex-crazed white men butchered and burned him because a young white woman revealed her love for Jeff.

Because Mama and I were at one point living in Indianapolis, which forty-odd years ago was rotten with Klan terror and violence, she would warn me constantly against the deadly danger of associating with white girls lest the dread hooded night riders come for her baby as they had for Jeff Jones.

Strangely, this black man who was slain before the turn of the last century became after a while a powerfully vivid figure in my mind. It was as if I had really known him long ago. I feel anger and tension and sorrow build inside me whenever I think about Thomas Jefferson Jones because maybe in my mind he's a gory symbol for the multitudes of lynched and barbequed blacks.

The terror that was Jones' must always be mine and every black man's, for ever since slavery the black beast with his mythic pelvic poetry and epic love bone has tormented the white man. Historically, white women have had a notorious curiosity about the ecstasy potential in the rod of the meek beast.

A trillion pink, alabaster and gold sex pots infest the billboards and our television screens. We are conned that the white woman is the universal and absolute beauty and sexual ideal. Sex hucksters assault and inflame the national psyche through the media of movies, stage, television, magazines, and in every other way a consumer buck can be latched on to.

Now, in sex-glutted, racist America, a new gutsy black man inspired by the brilliantly bold wings of Malcolm X has arisen like a black phoenix from the flames of fear and the ashes of his crushed manhood to fuck over the white man as never before.

This thrilling defiance of the repressive power structure has attracted new hordes of white women. The gut crux of the accelerating racial violence and injustice in America is the black man's rapidly expanding cult of courage and his discovery of the inner riches of black selfhood.

The pedestal reverence of white men (particularly in the deep South) for their women and their insane ritual of making the black man a disemboweled corpse are like hideous mirrors reflecting the white man's sexual agony and his paranoic terror of the mythic big black superdick having universal congress with the mythic white supercunt.

The black man has been the victim of these white sexual terrors since this country's post-slavery lynching bloodbath and into today's more subtle lynching by the courts and by hoodlum police. These long-term atrocities and dangers have had drastic effects upon the black man's sexual attitudes toward white women.

The black man is tormented, taunted, repelled and magnetized by the white sex phantom haunting his mind. Many black men must hate the white woman with the same ferocity with which they desire her; and even in her embrace, during instants of awareness, they must despise her whiteness and their own weakness.

For she is, after all, the pale, deadly symbol that can trigger a ghastly montage of gouged-out black sex organs, crushed, charred corpses swinging from crooked necks with purple tongues lolled out of lipless, madly staring deathheads.

Surely the majority of black men living with black women work for successful and satisfying relationships. Most are probably sound and satisfactory. But in many cases the black man's full love and appreciation for the beauty and value of the black woman is soured by his admiration and desire for the white woman. That the black woman has existed and survived in the tortured hurricane of confusion raging in the black man's psyche is proof of her terrific strength of character.

The effect of the greatly increased availability to black men of white females of all ages, sizes, types, sexual appetites and points of origin—from plush, white upper-class mansions to lopsided shacks in Appalachia—has been a stiffening of competition among black women for the few highly desirable, affluent black men, not to mention the great pool of physically attractive black men of modest means, and even the barroom and poolhall dudes.

It seems likely that soon the Beauty, the Sex Queen of phony nigger society, the high yellow, simulated, substitute white woman, will feel the red hot threat of the white temptress marring her arrogant facade.

Many of these neurotic yellow snobs with Cadillacs, minks and the grits and greens problem under control band together in major cities across the nation and form clubs with the tacit understanding that dark-skinned black women will be excluded or sharply limited in number. The effect of this black bigotry is that within so-called black society the dark-hued female, despite her virtues and attributes (she is still the overwhelming majority in black America) is virtually cancelled out as a prime marital target of top black business and professional men.

Because the high yellow most closely resembles the white woman, I and most black men all the way down to the gutters of black America have been conditioned to prefer the white woman or the lighter black woman to the darker for marriage or shack-up. And quite frequently and tragically, it is usually the darker sister who is seduced and impregnated with vicious hit-and-run con.

I believe that the lower sexual and beauty rating of the darker complexioned female by most black men is greatly responsible for her appearance in the overwhelming majority among armies of street hustlers in the many cities I have visited across the nation. Because she is an overshadowed underdog, essentially deprived of the chance to win herself a dependable, desirable man and thereby security and a sense of self-esteem, she is an easy mark for the gaudy black pimp and his hypnotic castles in the air.

Another interesting possibility is that the

black street whore perhaps has an unconscious motive when she works that area of the game. For there she has direct sexual contact with America's unchallenged symbol of wealth, influence and power: the white man. And she demands and gets paid for it.

The basic tension in the black woman's relationship with the black man is often centered in his psychological emasculation and in the black woman's reaction to his pain. She anguishes over his tragedy, and too often in unreasoning, cruel resentment she will praise the reputed superior virtues of white men, the hated cripplers of his manhood. She may goad him, prod him unmercifully to be a man and then, fearing his bloody destruction by racist cops and other killers stalking the ghettos, she will beg him not to rise up, not to be a man.

She is rewarded with the smoldering hostility of her man for her clumsy and painful attempts at therapy. And possession of the alabaster symbol of esthetic splendor and freedom, the white woman, becomes his dream, his obsession, for with her he can trample, stomp upon the traditions and rules of the white world. And perhaps within the pungent fire of her forbidden cunt he expects to burn away his secret self-hatred and find the glory of his manhood. By sexual conquest of the white woman, he can hurt and torment the white man and punish the unappreciative black woman.

My many years as a black pimp gave me an intimate, clear view (through my whores' recounting of the sexual antics of white men) of the twisted motivations that lie behind the white man's sexual hunger for black women. Not so odd (in view of the guilt factor) is the fact that the majority of white men who compulsively go into the treacherous ghettos on sex hunts are racists (most white men in America are).

Some of them prefer smooth-looking, well-groomed, clean girls for straight sex. Many will pay to verbally or sometimes physically abuse the girls. Others prefer the roughest, toughest and least clean girls in the streets on whom to perform cunnilingus, and in other frequent instances to wallow in defecation and to receive other forms of gross sexual punishment.

One effect of racism in America is to impose such an aura of vileness around sexual intercourse between white man (the racist) and black woman that he must regard her in his guilt and hostility as a sub-human animal, a mere garbage dump for his sperm and hostilities. The sadistic racist becomes the whimpering sexual masochist only because his guilt overwhelms his hatred for the black race. The racist submits his quivering body to the beatings and feces of the black woman. Eagerly, joyously, he roots his ecstatic nose into a black cunt to stain himself, punish himself. With balls near bursting, he will leave pleasant nests (and the alabaster supercunt) in suburbia to comb the booby-trapped ghetto for a black female object—his instrument of torture.

The white man is notorious for his "sock it in and run" treatment of black women. Relatively few white men take black women as mates. But thousands of white women marry black men. The arrangement is one of the most trying between two human beings.

The white woman so attached must renounce her whitehood for blackhood and literally become a nigger and all that it implies in racist America. She is shut off in most cases from relatives and friends, and marooned in an alien black world where true black friends are hard to come by. The black man is in the ironic position of possessing the symbol of freedom, yet he is hobbled and shackled by his blackness and must constantly guard against making his white mate the substitute object of his obsessive and smoldering hatred for the racist white man. The worst torment of all can be the gnawing suspicion that his woman is hating him for making a nigger of her and that she dreams secretly of fleeing the black world to return to the white world and a white man.

White women come to black men because they are guilt-ridden apologists for white racism. They come to offer a compassionate white bosom in penance; many are rebels thumbing noses at white social and sexual taboos. Some are derelicts, rebuffed by the white world and ego starved. They can be women who simply meet a black man and desire him, or they can be faddists doing the "in" thing of impaling themselves at least once on a mythic nigger love bone.

I do not believe that the effects of the black revolution will do more than increase the gravitation of white women to the sexual magnet, the new-dimensioned black man, and thereby further polarize the races and lure new recruits to the ranks of hard-core racists in America. The wild dreamers of the total integrationist dream (that one day a black man can, for instance, kiss his white wife on, say, a downtown street in Jackson, Mississippi, without being instantly torn to pieces) can be excused as they sheepishly slink away fifty or even a hundred years from now.

UNCLE TOM AND HIS MASTER IN THE VIOLENT SEVENTIES

Today's Uncle Tom and his master have not changed basically in philosophy, motivation and relationship since the days of slavery when the genuflective "House Nigger," the original Uncle Tom, flashed his pearly .32 and supported the white slave master's atrocities against the lives and minds and human rights of his own black kind.

Now, as then, Uncle Tom adores his master and often has great talent for mimicry of his idol which reveals his confusion and self-hatred.

Today's Uncle Tom is often not averse to peddling his daughter's virtue or ransoming his soul to the devil to own a house in ecstatic proximity to the Master. Masochistically he prefers the Master's watering and feeding places where he waits in catatonic terror for the inevitable outraged white soldier of segregation to lop off his quivering black balls with a verbal saber.

Until the kick-off of the violent phase of black revolution in Watts in 1965, Uncle Tom luxuriated in the approbation and confidence of the Master. The subsequent proliferation of violent black rebellion in Detroit, Newark, Chicago and elsewhere across America dramatically exposed the near worthlessness and obsolescence of political and religious Tom as an effective agent for the Master in his strategy to keep niggers nonviolent and peaceful in the ghetto torture chambers while Uncle Tom conned the masses that he was negotiating fruitfully with the Master and/or God, and everything was going to be all right pretty soon.

Tom's value to the Master plummets proportionally to the acceleration of loud mass dissent against poverty and racism and revolutionary violence in the black ghettos. And Tom in the violent Seventies will not only be treated with contemptuous disdain by the Master, but will like all blacks have no immunity to possible genocide or imprisonment in a concentration camp.

Uncle Tom comes forth in many hats and

shapes—politician, preacher, greedy, glory-grabbing nigger socialite and the plain power addict. But all are outlaw whores in the stable of the white power structure and suck a mixture of shit and money from the bung hole of the Master as the murderous noose of racism and poverty chokes their brethren.

I believe that many so-called black religious and political leaders start out with sincerity and a determination to help the black race in its struggle for justice and equality but are trapped and processed into Uncle Toms by cunning white politicians and a conditioned yen for "silken living." Of course there are blacks who successfully resist the process, but they usually suffer stunted careers and are shunted to oblivion by the Master.

An aristocratic character (a rich, white liberal politician) in a novel I once wrote graphically delineated the process when he boasted to a white conservative police chief about the master plan for the suppression of black freedom in America.

He said, "Pete, you're a fine policeman. I admire you greatly as such. But your political ideas are all wet. I'm going to give you a few political facts of life. But first, I must preface a bit.

"I, and at least ninety percent of the whites in this country with so-called liberal leanings privately wouldn't care a whit if all the niggers in America were herded into one of your larger canyons out West and then bombed into oblivion. However, we realize that the niggers are with us and lamentably will perhaps always be with us. You conservatives can't resist your childish displays of hostility.

"You are not aware of the master plan now in effect in these United States for the containment and control of the niggers. That master plan is in the competent hands of the liberal white leaders. They are the indispensable agents of the white race. It is they with their mastery of the base emotion, their sophisticated analysis of nigger psychology that permits them to project a merciful sympathetic image.

"This is vital so that harassed, beleagured nigger ministers and other black leaders can have such a source to which they can appeal. Pete, a four letter word is the key to the white master plan.

"That word is hope. It means that what is desired is obtainable. The human organism when deprived of it can become unpredictable, destructive, deadly. Pete, the liberals are aware that the great masses of niggers hope for escape from the ghettos.

"They want to spill over into the mainstream of American life and pollute it with their criminality and lust for our women. They want to rub elbows with us all. They want to lose the consciousness of their blackness at the expense of our culture and privacy. They want to contaminate our Anglo-Saxon bloodline.

"Pete, the fatal failing of the conservative is that he bluntly and stupidly strangles hope in the niggers. His rigid emotional structure won't let him practice the subtle arts of deception and guile. These are essential adjuncts in our strategy to lull, to keep alive hope in the nigger without making his wild dreams of freedom realities.

"You say we liberals have helped countless niggers to escape from the ghettos through appointive positions in government and industry. That we liberals put those white collars around their black necks, not the conservatives. That we betrayed the white race and let the niggers invade our white society. Pete, you're tragically misinformed. There are really two ghettos. One is physical, the other psychological. Now it is true that we have selected certain niggers to wear white collars.

Almost all of them do make physical escapes from the ghetto, with our assistance, of course. Our motives are first to give dramatic, well-publicized reinforcement to our liberal image.

"Secondly, those niggers whom we seem to liberate are precisely those types of niggers who possess rare intellect and academic polish. We have to remove them from the seething black masses. If we didn't they could conceivably give the mindless masses effective leadership against the white race.

"Now, the diametric differences between the nigger world and the white world afford us the devices by which we neutralize and defang the white collar escapees from the ghetto.

"The technique is roughly this. The freed nigger, elective and appointive as well, will face his entry into the white world with no little trepidation. His fears, his insecurity are born of the unfamiliar, unknown facets of the strange new world. Underlying all of this, of course, is his well-hidden but nonetheless strong sense of inferiority. His is an urgent, practical need, perhaps unconscious, to conform to the mores, the protocol of the new world. He has a deathly dread of conspicuous violation of these codes.

"His terror is that the whites who have sponsored him will take notice and hurl him back into the ghetto. He's compelled to emulate white emotional control and polished, patient conduct. We flatter him as he becomes more like us. His identity, his fiery racial resolutions, if he has any, fade and are eventually lost. If he fights the mold, we poke derisive fun at him and make him appear ludicrous. One can't act like a nigger in suave white surroundings.

"We listen with compassion to his now guilt-ripened pleas for help for his black brothers back in the ghetto. We throw him a few crumbs of appeasement. But soon he becomes worthless to them and priceless to us. He has lost his power to lead them, to hurt us. In his thinking and love for the creature comforts, he becomes one of our troops in all respects save for his blackness. He helps us to repress and enslave his own kind.

"You conservatives get uptight about sex between white tramps and niggers. Those girls are fecal matter, dregs, sediment settled at the bottom of the social barrel. Historically and appropriately, the sexual peccadillos of the dregs are the petty province of conservatives, red necks, white trash and other hysterical slobs. The typical flower of white womanhood by training and breeding would rather be dead than have sexual congress with a nigger. The niggers and the dregs will always be with us at the bottom of the barrel."

Uncle Tom's future in the Seventies looks bleak in the face of rising black militancy and its predictably punitive policy for blacks who delude and hustle other blacks in the ghettos. And the Master's future looks less than bright as he turns on his own white young like a rabid wolf to crush their dissent against racism, poverty and war.

Certainly much of the Master's monumental fury lies in his awareness that alarming numbers of young white people would love to defecate upon the graves of America's most illustrious heroes, past and present. The power structure's fear and rage and its irrational blanket vendetta of barbarism against the young dissenters and their mushrooming crop of elder sympathizers have driven the violent arm of the New Left underground.

Much of the Master's bestial cruelty toward his own white young is possibly rooted in the traumatic realization that, in the wake of the black revolution, young whites in alarming numbers have rapturously embraced the black life style–its soul-laced music, speech idiom and over-all social attitudes.

Certainly this wholesale imitation of and compassion for blacks would indicate an unprecedented and imminent possibility for wholesale sexual congress with blacks. The niggerization of his young has thrown the Master off balance not only because of his classic paranoiac concern for that mythic sanctity of white womanhood, but also because of a potential white coalition with the black revolution.

These of course are secondary fears plaguing the Master. His central fears are when and where the fanatical bombers of the New Left will strike and what is the true quantity and quality, ultimate objectives and specific location of the unpredictable enemy. And the Master's unease is compounded by the knowledge that his enemy, unlike the blacks, do not have high visibility and therefore enjoy the advantages of easy spying and casual, deadly access to the embattled environs of the power structure and the despised person of the Master.

The Master's dire situation has arisen not only because he offers no moral leadership, but because his use of repressive force instead of dialogue in dealing with young disenchanted Americans prevents him from examining and correcting the escalating rage and terror. A police state created ostensibly for the stomping down of the niggers and the New Left would soon become a horror state for all the people. Historically, in the face of repression beyond the limits of human endurance, the populace has risen up in general rebellion against a government ignorant of this fact.

The Master, the power structure, is diseased with such unreasoning cruelty, arrogance, fear and rage that in the violent Seventies it could well drown in its own blood.

ABOUT RAIN AND RAPPING WITH SWEETSEND PAPPY LUKE

Rain! Female Rain. How do you feel about her? I dig her. I can say that in a slightly special way. She's an old flame of mine. I discovered the femaleness of her while doing a bit with Sweetsend Pappy Luke in the federal joint at Leavenworth, Kansas, long ago. As night cell-house orderly, I was free to stop outside Pappy's cell and rap about the gungho freak broads we had known. That first spring in the joint was probably the rainiest in Kansas history. Pappy would often gaze up at the opened barred windows near the cell-house ceiling and say, "Slim, listen! She's out there thrashing and sighing and stinking like a broad in heat."

On many rainy nights, I'd go down the tier to my cell with my balls burning with fever and aching with pressure. There were a half-dozen cells where two packs of butts could summon a pink puckered anus bud to press eagerly against the bars for a guy's blood-swollen organ to rip off. But I would go lie in the quiet gloom of my cell with the terrible convict hunger for the presence and odor of a female. I'd close my eyes, flog my monster, and inhale the scent of the rain and imagine it was the raw perfume of a hot lubricating bitch. And there in loneliness and fantasy it was true. The rain was a woman.

Sweetsend Pappy Luke got his monicker hung on him by his con men associates because of his skill and artistry in putting his con victims on the "send" for their bread and for the eagerness with which they brought back their dough to the grifting palm of Pappy Luke. The Pappy part of his monicker was because his hair turned silvery in his late twenties.

We continued our friendship in Chicago in the mid-forties when we finished our bits. But eventually a con man has to get in the wind or take a fall. So we lost touch in '50.

Pappy surfaced in October of '67 several days after I had briefly plugged a book on the late Louis Lomax show on L.A.'s KTTV. He had conned the station for my number and we both were happy as hell to be in touch again. He was in his late eighties, but the sinewy body was uncurved and the sable eyes in the black-hawk face still flashed fire. He was squared up with a comfortable income from real estate, but he was as hot as a flimflammed hooker holding a queer sawbuck in her mitt after giving a trip around the world. He was convinced I got only six minutes on the tail end of the Lomax show because I was an ex-pimp and he figured black middle-class Lomax was responsible. I begged him to forget it but he sent the man a soul-stomping wire accusing him of bias against a brother.

Pappy became a great friend and fan as the next few years passed. It was like the peppery old guy had adopted me and, like a father, was vicariously living my ups and downs in the writing game. I didn't fight the situation, I enjoyed the colorful old guy's company and friendship. But one rainy day he came to visit and in the excitement and heat of a rap session the old man almost burst his pump.

I think Pappy's visit was in the first week of January of 1971. Well anyway, it was shortly after James Farmer hobbled out of Nixon's stable of whores in quest of his lynched manhood. I was sitting in the living room watching the rain through the open door as her trillion jeweled feet danced on the mirrored asphalt, when Pappy's red Riviera pulled up in front. I started to get up to take an umbrella down the walk. But before I could get in gear he had sprung from the Buick and was hot-footing it toward the front door like a guy propelled by a fresh jolt of cocaine. He only grunted when I spoke and took his white raincoat at the door. He was grimly clutching a rolled newspaper.

Pappy sat with tight jaws on the sofa facing my easy chair. He was slit-eyeing me and banging the paper club against his thigh. I guessed that some square joker or cop had fouled his mood. I squirmed and opened with, "How about a cup of coffee to help you get yourself together?" He flashed a quicksand con smile and chanted, "Mister Slim, Luke is together now, has been together for almost a century, and is going to stay together." Then with his face aimed down at the rolled paper in his fist, he suddenly zoomed his eyes upward and stared accusingly at me from the top of his head. I knew the old guy was really salty with me when he came on with the formal "Mr. Slim" bit. I rifled through my mind for some promise I hadn't kept. The slate was clean so I said, "What's wrong, Pappy? What the hell do you think I've done to you?"

He violently unrolled the newspaper and hurled a copy of a famous mass circulation news magazine rolled inside it onto my lap. In a breaking voice he said, "How could you sucker off for that conniving white broad and let her dupe you into the fairytale bullshit in that magazine? After using you the lousy white folks wouldn't even mention that you write books and that you pulled yourself out of the gutter. Chump, why didn't you ever crack to me that this broad interviewed you? Mark, you need to get yourself together if you were that desperate!"

I had been speedreading the short article while Pappy was tongue-whacking me. It was about a white dancer who reportedly did her topless-bottomless thing in a San Francisco watering hole for mostly black pimps and whores. She sometimes bared her thicket for a double sawbuck a night and burgled gems of the pimp game from forty pimp skulls toward a Ph.D. and a professorship in anthropology. The piece was crutched and flawed by the usual contrived soul shit that white writers and Ivory Tower black scribes use when writing about street Niggers. Some of the observations from my book, *Pimp,* were quoted in the piece. And the piece claimed that the dancer had interviewed me extensively. I had neither heard of her nor seen her in my life.

I put the magazine on the table beside me, looked right into his eyes and said, "Pappy, I never gave that woman an interview. I didn't know she existed until you lugged that magazine in here. Do you believe me?"

The sable eyes X-rayed me for a long, tense moment before he nodded. Then he leaned toward me and said gravely, "Son, what are you going to do about it?"

I said, "What can I do? Everybody I could beef to would be white. Do you believe the magazine publisher or the courts would care a good goddamn that she sliced off a hunk of my black ass? Pappy, let's have coffee and a few hands of rap rummy. It isn't really important. I could forget her and the piece in five minutes if you tossed it out of your mind. C'mon, what do you say, pal?"

He leaned back against the sofa and said softly, "Mister Slim, do you know why that white broad is so important that we can't throw her out of our minds?"

I said, "You swindled thousands of suckers and I took lots of good bread from bad girls.

So why are your balls in the fire about some white woman gaming for a Ph.D? You sound like a holy roller. I'm not ecstatic about the shabby way she handled my name and my work. But she happened to me, Pappy, me. And I can forget her if I want to. I'm not your child. If you just can't make it without a son to push around, why in the hell don't you adopt one?"

He got to his feet and stood over me wagging a heavy index finger near my face. The hatchet face was drawn rigid, embalmed in anger and hurt and the artery at the side of his neck was a ballooned cable of leaping blood. The strangling sounds in his throat stopped and he shouted, "You don't have to remind me that a lop-eared sucker like you is not my kid. A son of mine wouldn't need his coat yanked to rags before he woke up to the fact that that nickel slick white broad is really only a petty part of a nit shit vicious link in the criminal chain of white fraud and robbery of black people's labor, talent, folklore and creativity—ever since this sanctuary for top echelon white thieves and murderers was founded. Your pimp brain can't grasp that the white broad stole something from you and those black pimps in San Francisco more precious than money.

"No, you couldn't be my son. A son of mine would know, for instance, the connection between that white broad and the black men who bled artistry and talent behind the scenes so Benny Goodman could masquerade as the King of Swing. You see and hear big star white broad singers playing soul and blues con on stage, TV and in movies. Do you feel pleasure? Or anything at all? Mr. Slim, I feel pain. I hurt when I hear them.

"I remember black singers Ma Rainey and Bessie Smith and their struggle and tragedy and dreams unrealized. I remember that army of white singers all the way back to Sophie Tucker that aped the style and flair of Ma and Bessie to enjoy the glory and luxury of true stardom denied our sisters because they were black. Mr. Slim, you still think that white broad is unimportant?"

His face went to a sudden grayish pallor and tiny diamonds of sweat popped out on his forehead. He swayed and gulped for air. I leaped up and eased him down on the sofa. I got an icy towel and bathed his brow. I took his shoes off and gave him some brandy. Sliding my chair close to the sofa, I said softly, "I bought the convincer, Pappy. You're right all the way. Okay?"

Pappy pushed himself up to a sitting position on the sofa. His color was good and except for his hand trembling as he took a sip of brandy, he seemed together.

I said, "Pappy, I'm sorry I cracked tough on you. I feel like a . . ."

Pappy furiously jiggled his palms before my face and growled, "You stop playing that chump con on me. Only sucker friends need to give and gobble apology for telling the truth about each other."

I said, "What the hell was it that slugged you, your pump?"

He shrugged and muttered, "A lot of mileage and a little indigestion. Now let's forget about it. You think the white folks booted you in the butt? Let me show you how a so-called 'enlightened' black newspaperman handled you and those black scufflers in San Francisco."

Pappy scooped the rolled-up newspaper off the floor and started to flatten it out on the sofa. I noticed it was an edition an enraged black pimp named "Drawback" had shown me the night before. The paper carried the reaction of a black columnist to the newsmagazine's write-up of the San Francisco black pimps and whores.

I watched warily as Pappy flipped pages for the column. His jaws were tight again and I felt he could probably get mad enough to maybe bust a heartstring if he caught me in slumber on any heavy social or racial issue in the paper. He shoved the paper double-folded onto my lap. I said, "Drawback let me peek at it last night."

Pappy dipped his platinum top toward the paper and said, "Slimmy, I'm old as fornication, and I've been in and out and around the 'Horn of Life and Plenty' more times than this chump has been laid. Even now, today, you could shove us both into the street to just hustle from the raw nub, and I'd show you a grand for every nickel of his!"

I said, "Pappy, let's not get emotional just because some black writer can't put together an air castle for a whore, or tell a ten grand lie to a mark."

Pappy frowned and growled, "Well, what do you think of that hate piece?"

I said, "Give me a minute." I read the writer's blasting of the black pimps and whores up San Francisco way as sick criminals and as a splotch on humanity. Then I stared at the image of the pleasant-faced gentleman near the top of his column peering with bright, alert eyes through heavy glasses. I remembered how I had enjoyed his excellent stories on sports and its black stars, and also his poignant etchings of Los Angeles' Central Avenue back in its bawdy days of glory. I remembered how a colleague and friend of the columnist once lauded him in his column as the "Henry Aaron of Journalism," and as a "compassionate Good Samaritan" with a beautifully broad understanding; as a fearless writer "with the guts to call it as he sees it."

Then I thought about murdered Black Panther leader Fred Hampton in Chicago and slaughtered Jerry Aimee and Leonard Deadwyler and many other black victims executed by the police. I was vainly searching my memory to recall an occasion when this same black columnist had blasted polemic fury about the criminals in blue when Pappy slapped my knee and said impatiently, "Damn, Slimmy, you read slow!"

"I was thinking, Pappy," I answered him. "It seems like he's about to bust wide open with hate for black pimps and whores." And while Pappy scowled and prepared a withering rejoinder to my weak remark, I thought how the whole episode was really significant only as another symptom of the divisiveness and class mania that have hacked Black America into hating, bitter fragments and maimed its struggle for freedom and justice.

"Pappy," I told the old man, "we have to

try to understand this gentleman so we can understand his whole cult. Pappy, even ex-hustlers like ourselves have to confess that black pimps and whores ain't into no Martin Luther King and Mary McLeod Bethune bags out in those streets. But Pappy, I'm wondering what besides guts does a black gentleman with a solid reputation for compassion and understanding have or lack to publicly stomp on black victims of the poisonous American Dream? What kind of intellectual glaucoma afflicts a respected black gentleman so as to allow him to passionately 'see' and flay black pimps and whores as criminals, while fiends in blue bloodlet in the black ghetto unseen and uncondemned in his column as the criminal terrorists they are?"

Pappy took a sip of brandy and said, "Slimmy, maybe his paper muzzles him on cops. And what the hell, there's little risk in kicking the asses of a crew of black scufflers who have a bitch of a time just staying out of the joint and corraling a fast buck.

"Slimmy, let's take a look at this joker and his cult in a basic way. I'm going to take it for granted that his Mama didn't dump him into a trash can like happened to me when I was two days old, or that his old man didn't bounce him against the wall and cop a heel like happened to you when you were six months old."

Pappy tented manicured fingers beneath the cleft in his chin and continued.

"Slimmy, Ivory Towers are really prisons and a joker's mind can become sealed into one brick by brick sometimes from his childhood. You can usually tell when a joker is all locked in when he has conned himself that he is so pure high up there above sin and corruption that even his asshole has the fragrance of a gardenia. He glares down at the spermy sinners funning and sucking beneath him and flies into a slobbery rage. Like Christ Almighty himself he wails and pretends to suffer for the imagined shame of a whole race. But deep down in a secret chamber of his being he is really outraged because he's sealed himself up in his Ivory prison.

"I remember 'way back when I was a tender buck how jokers like him and his cult appeared to the general public as understanding humanitarians and champions of black advancement. Sometimes they do help and advance a certain type of black person and they fart in righteous condemnation of bigotry in any form. But, Slimmy, ain't they so poisoned with bias and bigotry for other types of black people that their public images are a fraud and their lives a lie?

"Can any black man really be a leader, a humanitarian and champion of black advancement who tries only to understand and help the progress of those blacks who he probably believes will become social mock-ups of himself? Slimmy, I don't want to get carried away like a sucker. But if this joker and his cult are not what they appear to be, then they are fakes, social grifters playing the con for honor and respect from the public that they don't deserve. And the great tragedy about them and us is that we can't link arms in the death struggle of our race."

"Right on, Pappy!" I said, slapping his outstretched palm. "But Pappy, how in the hell can you get it across a barrier like that to the man and his cult the fact of the kinship of all black people, including himself, as nigger victims and targets for repression and murder in America?"

Pappy glanced at his wristwatch and stood up. "I don't have the answer. And you and I will be dead and stinking before those black jokers wake up to the fact that they are not special human beings to the white man, not even special niggers when the life-and-death chips are down. Those black jokers ain't going to get out of those Ivory prisons until the day the murderers come for them. Like I said, they're bricked in there in sweet slumber, terrified of pain, suffering and dying, and most of all they fear loving the black militant strugglers and street nigger losers 'way down there in the gutter beneath them—because they know the gimlet eye of their white power idols is watching. Slimmy, I could cry like a crumb crusher about it. But I won't. I've got some sinning to do with a young Creole broad and I'm fifteen minutes late right now. Thanks for everything and later, Slimmy, later."

He scooped up his coat and, throwing it cape-style across his proud shoulders, went down the walk. I watched him gun the crimson Riviera away in the rain. I sank back into my easy chair. I was all alone again except for the rain out there still dancing her heart out. I closed my eyes and inhaled her wild perfume and let her whispery voice gentle and soothe me like the broad, like the sweet bitch she is.

AN OPEN LETTER TO ICEBERG SLIM

New York, N.Y.

January 10, 1970

Dear Iceberg Slim:

After having virtually memorized your three books, I decided I could come to you as you came to Sweet Jones in *Pimp* for advice, to get my "coat pulled." Iceberg, I am not insane, nor am I mentally ill. Not any of that heavy drama. But ever since I got back to the States last year from Nam, I have been unable to find the key to an understanding of myself and of my place in the world about me and of even a way to help my black brothers and sisters. Sometimes when I really try hard to think out solutions to my problems, my mind seems to break up like the pieces of a jigsaw puzzle. I could get hooked up with some of my mother's well-off relatives right here in New York tomorrow. But when I got back from Nam, I chose to make it on my own in Harlem and pull out of this ghetto on my own some day.

Maybe I can't get my head together, because before I went to Nam when I was eighteen, I had never been away from home. I come from a large city in the deep South. My old man is a bigshot nigger down there who is so brainwashed by whitey's bullshit that he threw a big thing, a hundred people, to celebrate my going to murder little yellow people in Nam. Mama was different, she hated war and always worried that some day I would have to go. She died when I was sixteen. Iceberg, I was so square before I got to Nam, you wouldn't believe. I thought hash was what went with biscuits, and that before you got in a chick's pants you bought rings and a piece of paper.

But I changed in Nam, and I am a man now, and whatever happens I am never going back to my father's house and to all his nigger society, Uncle Tom crap. I admire you, Iceberg, because you didn't grin and

Uncle Tom to escape from the ghetto. You wrote your way out. Iceberg, I have a strong desire to become a writer. I believe it could be the salvation of my head and I could help my people. I have been writing down some of my experiences in Nam and about how we nigger grunts were treated by our white superior officers. You wouldn't believe the jive scene over there. One afternoon after we had been out on 36 hour patrol and fought through several ambushes by Charlie, we dragged our raunchy asses to some cover and collapsed. My best pal had been blown apart by a mine and I had been wounded when one of those shiny star fairies from D.H.Q. dropped in on a chopper for a hot minute. That white mother stood no more than four feet from me spouting the usual off the wall shit. I looked at his boots and you wouldn't believe, they were so clean and gleaming I could actually see my reflection on them. Something came over me and I was shaking with the impulse to blow that grinning mother out of his shiny boots with a burst from my rife.

Iceberg, I feel used up, tricked and confused. I have killed and I found out it's no big thing to kill or die. I'm not afraid of the devil. I want to be a writer. I want to help my people. I have been writing down some part of the now scene. I want to cast off this jigsaw thing inside my head and relate clearly to what's happening to black people. If I flunk out as a writer then I will try to fit in some other way, even pick up a gun and join the revolution.

Iceberg, you wouldn't believe the articles and stuff I have read on what type of writing a black writer should be concerned about. You know the old hassle about protest stuff and literary art. I would appreciate it very much if you could find time to write me a short note of advice about the writing game.

Respectfully,

W. N.

Dear Brother,

I am answering your letter in the early hours of the morning. Brother, the pain of your confusion and frustration, your hurt as a black man in America, seem so much like my own feelings long ago, except that at your age I was too street poisoned, was perhaps not intelligent enough to sense my need for new values and for advice.

Brother, you have come to me in your unhappiness like a son needing advice and comfort from his father, and I feel proud and deeply touched that you did. But I also feel sadness at the nagging thought that I am too new from the blind mist, too battered, still too unhealed to rise fully to your needs and image of me.

Perhaps I can best advise you by pulling your coat to some personal things about my present life-style and some deep feelings and impressions I have as a writer and as an older black brother and nigger in this society. I hope I can give you a clearer, perhaps less painful view of yourself and of our bittersweet ghetto.

Brother, I live in the ghetto and have no desire to break its bonds, for I am after all a street nigger learning to write, who is incidentally being blessed with an increasing audience for his efforts. Materially, I dream at the moment of more living space and less wobbly furniture. I experience and view the ghetto as a savagely familiar place of spiritual warmth rich in the writer's treasure of pathos, conflict and struggle. I am convinced that for me it was the only place where I could discover and keep an awareness of who I really am and where I could find my haven, my purpose as a writer and a nigger in this criminal society.

Brother, I fear to flee to some other strange, plush ghetto where I would possibly be marooned among glossy, status-shit fanatics whom I would have to ape for acceptance. Once long ago in my tender stage, I did time in the showplace dungeon of a foxy black socialite located in an exclusive interracial compound in the East. Dear Brother, the week I served with that gushy manic depressive phony and her interracial horde of Ivory Tower rectums seemed longer and tougher than any bit I ever served in a real joint. I know that only in some black ghetto can my street nigger soul soar, stay proud and pure and unfucked-over.

Brother, I hope that at this point you still consider me a success. Now just for the sake of finding something useful in another direction, let's look at a much different kind of black writer, say one from a lifelong middle-class background, whose writings you admire and respect because you are a different kind of brother. Like a certain older black writer whose writings are virtually unknown to the black masses, I am gifted, craven, cunning or perhaps simply repressed enough to have created a novel dealing with the condition of blacks in America that has won admiration from some white critics and charms even the white racist. "Magnificently detached and objective," "unmatched aloofness from bitterness and accusation," say the white critics in gratitude for unpricked conscience. And the white racists will spread the word, "The Nigger is a genius . . . ," "What a truthful look into the black ghetto," to close with the final, damning, "He writes like a white man."

Watch out! Take my hand, young Brother, as we avoid that gilded glob of bullshit about the ideal of the colorless black writer and the superiority of his purely objective art. I believe that in these times a black writer is a success only when the black masses can relate to his work and to him with respect and a strong sense of kinship. I believe a black writer in these times who shuns or loses kinship with his people is early doomed to dry up and die as a writer. He needs for his creative survival a living, throbbing lifeline to his people, for with only the impersonal white critics' cold pats on his nappy head and the fawning quicksand favor of the white public, his writer's juices will drain away. It has apparently happened recently to the most brilliantly articulate black writer in the history of American literature. The fake fire in his sweet philosophy of love and understanding for our genocidal enemies exiled him a trillion spiritual miles away from the cold rage of the awakening black masses to an intellectual island prison. The fickle white critics now ignore him or come only to maim and defame him, to gleefully stomp the corpse of his creative work.

Brother, what do you think? What kind of writer do you want to be, that you want the world to hear and pay attention to? And just as important, will you become a victim of this nigger-killer society, or survive as a fighter at some level of the struggle for black freedom? Brother, to survive we must strip our total beings of any boob black bourgeoisie values and creampuff attitudes toward the horror in America which we might have absorbed. Only then can we become aware of the hideous truth that every male human born into this society with black skin is a target for physical or psychological murder or for the kind of sinister mental plague which turns out the kind of nigger robot who strives and hungers for the approval and favor of his enemies. He defends and softens their crime against the black race with kinky bull shit on TV and in the black press. From his fat gut he foul-mouths the wine and dope shattered victims of racism in the black ghetto as "lazy leeches" and young black revolutionaries as suicidal scum. His diseased mouth and pen build hot air monuments to himself and other white power structure black whores as proof that any determined nigger can become a success in this society.

Brother, we cannot survive, we will never be free unless we make ourselves immune to confusion, to the diseased rhetoric of certain so-called black leaders. At this instant my ear is catching a TV interview with a famous and fluent black victim of brainwashing, doing his robot bit on the TV screen before me. Brother, I wish you could watch and listen to this robot bit with me for a moment. I wish you could watch this black brother and listen to him not with hate or rage but with understanding and sympathy. But most urgently with the realization that he is our enemy by the unshakable equation that a defender unwitting or not is our enemy—an ally and friend of our enemy cannot be other than our enemy. I hurt deeply for him and for us as I watch and listen.

The white interviewer leans forward toward our dapper gray-thatched brother who blinks owlishly through stylish bifocal windows. The question—"Do you as a black leader consider Mr. Nixon and his administration indifferent to the problems and needs of your race or perhaps even racist in attitude?"—has apparently insulted and shocked our brother. He winces and draws himself away from the beetle-browed white man with the indignation of a hundred-buck whore cringing away from a two-buck offer for a trip around the world.

The brother recovers quickly and stares toward the ceiling for a long moment while presumably his fifty-grand education and lackey purpose frame a defense for the pygmy president who has brought this nation to the brink of racial and economic destruction. Ah! He has it together. The velvet voice flows smoothly in an alibi that Nixon himself would applaud: "I have no conviction that Mr. Nixon and his administration are indifferent to black progress or are racist in nature. I think it very probable that Mr. Nixon, who is primarily a political animal, is understandably giving top priority at this time to political strategy and fence mending."

The liberal white interviewer frowns and says, "What are your feelings about the complaints of a number of black leaders that Mr. Nixon's ear and presence are virtually inaccessible for serious discussion of their people's problems?" Wistfully, the brother tells now about an occasion when he and other blacks were lathered in Nixon's charm at the White House and how it wouldn't have been good manners to sour the social cream with serious talk about black problems. Now the brother is saying sweetly, "But I do not believe the problem of serious access to Mr. Nixon is due to any indifference or racism on his part, but only to the sensible obligation of the men around Mr. Nixon to shield and protect him from as much pressure and unpleasantness as possible." Brother, I turned off the TV set. Perhaps time and the breed's zero-worth to us or the enemy will put it out of its misery.

Dear Brother, I hope I have cleared away some of your confusion. I hope you will understand that the real borderlines to struggle across, the real walls to break through are not without but within our own minds. Because we are black and we are forced to struggle with gun or pen or in some effective way for survival, for honor, for our manhood and for our escape from the painful mental ghetto of the uncommitted nigger in this criminal society.

But jumping into the violent revolutionary

movement at this time would be similar to an angry warrior challenging the enemy army with a brick-bat. Get involved with the ghetto struggle. Help your people to struggle.

And write, Brother, write. Don't ever want to live for yourself alone. The pimp life trapped me in that awful, empty bag for a quarter of a century. Brother, you've got the guts. You can do anything you want to. And please remember that any advice, knowledge or encouragement I can offer you as a writer and a black brother are there for you to draw from.

Sincerely yours,

Robert Beck
(Iceberg Slim)

ICEBERG ADRIFT: MUSINGS, LAMENTATIONS

One evening in the middle of June, 1970, my nightly three mile walk was unexpectedly delayed by the Elmer Gantry antics of America's foremost entrepreneur of the religious extravaganza. He appeared with his accomplices in a special video flimflam staged with the precision and cold-blooded objectivity of a top con mob. For an ex-street creature like myself, the spectacle of such an air-tight "game" was comparable to a religious fanatic's hallucination of the second coming of Christ.

I sat watching in amazement and reluctant admiration as our Presidential pygmy introduced America's wizard of worship, Dr. Billy Graham. To further heighten my amazement (and blood pressure), one of the great beloved ladies of the black race, Miss Ethel Waters, appeared also to express her love for America's youthful dissenters. Only to later tell the television multitudes how she would like to smack these dissenters for opposing the policies of her "precious child," Richard Milhous Nixon, close friend and political ally of racist Senator Strom Thurmond of South Carolina.

Fortunately I was aware that the principles of con are basically the same on every level. It looked to me like Dr. Graham, fall guy for the military-industrial establishment's carnage-steeped Asian adventures and burgeoning white hope for America's racists, sought through his video presence to camouflage and purify the Nixon administration's repressive, racist, war-hawk image in the poignant aura of Mammyism and a religious crusade.

Going out into the ghetto night on my walk, I thought of the ironic plight of Miss Ethel Waters. She had everything—talent, beauty, charm, one of the most bewitching voices in the history of show biz—to ensure her emotional and financial security in the winter of her life; everything except a white skin in racist America.

I lamented that instead of giving her the

respect that, as an enshrined black heroine of American Theater, she deserves, cunning white men have seized on her emotional unfulfillment and professional frustrations to exploit her as a maudlin, ethnic attraction in their buck-snatching roadshows.

Several blocks from home I walk into a drug store and immediately am confronted by an excited, slender black guy with chain-gangs and inferno cotton fields in his face and voice.

"Please suh, gimme uh ten cent piece," he blurts.

Instantly, I put it in his palm because his act is either real or such realistic con that it's worth a dime anytime. He whirls and goes pell mell toward a trio of public telephones; a pompous-looking old white guy in rimless bifocals is just leaving one.

As I pass them, the brother from big foot country is holding out a dime and asking the old white guy, "Ah ain't good at them numbers on thet phone. Please, suh, call the po-leece cuz mah crazee cuzun is gotta butcher knife 'roun unc's house an' he gonna . . ."

As I walk by, he thanks his benefactor for making the call and grins at me. But what the hell, I rejoice because my nigger-hood, fortunately, is together enough that I feel neither contempt nor irritation because he has by implication thought me not as competent as the white guy to operate the intricate telephone dial. For I know why he feels that way and how he got that way, and I smile and pat his shoulder as I pass him.

Halfway through the walk a two-man L.A.P.D. cruiser moves close to the curb and dogs my footsteps for a block. I remember that recently L. A. P. D. Homicide Lt. Robert Helder was quoted in newspapers as terming the murder of Jerry Lee Amie a "mistake, an unfortunate accident." Jerry died when four cops pumped twenty-five bullets into the unarmed victim right on his front lawn, in full view of his mother.

I keep walking and visualize Jerry Amie standing helplessly (drunk, according to the police) as his mother screams at the cops not to kill him. Although I am nauseously square and straight now, icy feet of apprehension stomp up and down my spine. I am unarmed and my followers are the heartless, unpredictable enemy, possibly killers with blood lust at peak cycle who might perversely halt and hassle me into a bullet-ripped corpse in the gutter. The gimlet-eyed pressure and the vivid picture of Jerry Amie are too much; I flee into a greasy spoon for coffee.

Standing, I put a quarter in front of my empty coffee cup as two dapper young black dudes get in my face.

One says, "Ice, pull this mark's coat that when you was rapping in your book *Pimp* about the whore game was a skull game, that you didn't mean sucking a cunt."

I patiently explain that I didn't, and I give them a standard pitch to dissuade them from the pimp game and all other criminal enterprises. But I can tell I'm not moving them. Both are already street poisoned.

I stop in a liquor store for gum. When I get back on the sidewalk, two husky young guys with hard faces stop me and ask how to get to the city of Compton. I am giving them a rundown when several young guys in a car pull to the curb. The driver gets out and walks over and says, "Is everything all right, Iceberg?" I tell him everything is cool and slap his palm as we split.

A block from home I go into a phone booth and stand for a moment looking at the receiver dangling off the cradle. I look about through the booth glass for some prior user. Lifting the receiver I listen for a live connection. I don't hear anything, so I drop a dime and start to dial. There is a nerve-grinding squeal of brakes and a heavy-set black guy with murder pulsing in his blood-shot eyes leaps from a jalopy and charges the phone booth. He punches the booth door open with the heel of his fist and buries his other hand ominously in his trouser pocket. He stands there with tiny bubbles of spittle nested in the corners of an angry mouth glaring at me.

He shouts, "Motherfucker, didn't you see the phone off the hook?"

Like I said, I was unarmed, and I am not a prize fighter. Surprise fighter, yes. So I open with strategic idiom.

I say, "Brother, I didn't see you around. And you ain't blowed the dime. What do you want to do, take this dime and use the phone now? Or do we chump off and send each other's nigger ass to the joint or the morgue about this white man's chickenshit phone?"

He blinks and some of the menace goes out of his eyes as he cocks his head to one side and says, "Nigger, don't I know you?"

I move out of the tight trap of the phone booth and say, "No, brother, I don't think so."

Then he grins and slams me hard against the shoulder. "Nigger, you're Iceberg Slim! I got one of your books where you're on the back squatting down like taking a crap. Shit! I know you, nigger."

Then he looks sheepish and says, "Slim, I been fighting that whiskey and having trouble with a skunk bitch. I got to come to myself, I guess."

He takes a snub-nosed .38 from his trouser pocket and throws it under his car seat. He offers to let me use the phone first, but I decline, slap his palm and cross my fingers as I set out to walk that last block home. I visualize the potential carnage and feel glad that I didn't act like an uptight, white-styled, middle-class black spouting indignation when the disturbed brother burst into that phone booth.

Several days after the phone booth adventure, I hear angry voices while cooling off on the sofa near an open window. I raise my glance up over the window sill and see a young black father in soiled Marine Corps fatigue pants arguing with an older, powerfully-built black guy over blocking the younger guy's driveway with his car. The older guy spews a blast of profanity and hurls himself into his machine. The young guy lounges coolly by the side of his own car watching his opponent shudder the sultry air as the car engine bellows into life.

Tons of hurtling steel bear down on the young guy, but not one hair of his Afro natural moves as the steel monster in passing grazes his clothing. He remains weirdly immobile, like some bronze heroic statue in a sleepy town square, even as the squawking tires bomb his face and sparkling clean car with the grit of the driveway. His animated eyes glow and pulse like black fire.

The older guy jumps from his machine in the street and races to the trunk. A female companion leaps out behind him and tearfully tries to dissuade him from opening the trunk, where perhaps he has stashed some deadly weapon.

The younger guy explodes into action and speeds down the driveway in his car. As he passes the struggling couple, he says with eerie sweetness, "Don't split, baby. I'll be right back."

The older guy gesticulates and prances about for a few seconds before roaring away. Before the racket of his leaving has died, the young guy wheels back into his driveway, and within ten minutes starts to hose down his car. The older guy barrels back seconds later and stands menacingly in the street glaring up the driveway at the young guy, who steps away from cover to stand defiantly staring at his opponent.

There is a patient, ominous looseness in the young guy's body, like that of killer gun slingers in the Old West. As he slouches there with hands on hips, I notice a curvy bulge at his belt line near the small of his back above the flowing tail of his shirt. The cemetery radiations from the young guy are so powerful that the older guy lets himself be persuaded by a pal to cop a heel after a bit of half-hearted threats and profanity.

Fortunately in this set-to between black men, there was no bloodshed. But usually the tragic reverse is true. It is not surprising that black men imprisoned in the ghettos of America use one another as substitute objects upon which to vent the rage and hatred they feel for the white man.

I am still cooling it on the sofa when a dear old friend, an elderly domestic worker, comes to visit. She has a decision to make and she wants advice. She is excited because she has received a letter from a so-called black man of God who virtually promises to wipe away all earthly problems for her, if she will send to an Eastern post office box a donation of ten to one hundred dollars for a prayer cloth.

Religious hustlers white and black suck the sweat and blood money from superstitious, elderly ghetto residents and from poor whites. These vultures have talents and morals inferior even to those of admitted hustlers and con men in the street. The pimp at least victimizes alert young people who conceivably will have time left in life to cast off the pimp's evil spell and to recoup financially and emotionally. The con man bilks victims who are not paupers and who are looking for something for nothing. In my opinion even the force-oriented character of the stickup man is superior to that of the craven religious hustler. The bandit puts his life on the line and faces his usually armed victim baldly and boldly and with noble recklessness.

The religious shark preys on the poor, the lame, the blind, the hopeless, the aged, the near senile, the sick, the dying. He shoots fish in a barrel. He hasn't the guts and intellect to go out and play his con against some kind of threat, challenge and risk. And he is so limited, so bereft of creative ideas, he has to use God as a prop.

My dear friend handed me the prayer cloth letter. It read:

"HOW TO USE THE PRAYER CLOTH:

"The Prayer Cloth may be laid upon the sick, placed in the bed, or carried on the person. It may also be used in other ways, and for many kinds of blessings as your faith may direct you. As you use the Prayer Cloth, think in your mind that this represents me, the MAN OF GOD, laying my hands upon you and praying the prayer of faith for you. EXPECT the answer as you use the Prayer Cloth. In fact, if you believe, the Prayer Cloth will be just like the hands of Jesus being laid upon you!

"One Prayer Cloth may be cut into many small pieces, and used in many different places, or by many different people. EVERY THREAD is blessed by prayer and faith in Jesus' name.

"FOR PEACE OR A BLESSING IN THE HOME—Place the Prayer Cloth in some secret place in the home. It represents the prayers of the MAN OF GOD for your home, and the presence of God to bless your home.

"IT DOES NOT MATTER HOW SOILED OR WORN the Prayer Cloth gets, it still brings results if used in faith. It may be washed if desired.

"FOR FINANCIAL OR MATERIAL BLESSINGS it may be carried in the purse or pocket book. Carry it when you go looking for a job, or to transact business, or to court. It will represent the presence and power of God going with you in these matters.

"FOR THE SALVATION OF LOVED ONES, AND THE DELIVERANCE OF THOSE WITH BAD HABITS LIKE DRINKING, USING DOPE, ETC.—Place the Prayer Cloth or a piece of it under, in or about their beds, or wherever they sleep, or wherever they SHOULD be sleeping. Let it be a secret. I gave one lady a Prayer Cloth for her husband who was drinking badly and told her to put it under his mattress. She came back later and said, "I placed the Cloth under my husband's mattress and he quit drinking, but he found the Prayer Cloth and went back to drinking!" So let this be a secret.

"THOSE WHO WANT TO STOP USING TOBACCO—Carry or keep the Prayer Cloth on you where you usually keep tobacco, and trust God to take the desire away.

"PLEASE, PLEASE, DO NOT SEND ANY CLOTH OR ANYTHING TO BE BLESSED. LET ME SEND YOU MY OWN PRAYER CLOTH AND BLESSINGS."

I advised my old friend until my voice got hoarse against sending part of her rent money for the prayer cloth. Finally, reluctantly, she agreed that in view of her great faith in God, buying a prayer cloth from a far-off stranger would really be an indictment of that faith and a painful extravagance.

Mama's warmth, inner beauty, intelligence, sweetness and thoughtfulness as a mother and human being are reflected in old letters, photographs and other dusty memorabilia she had hoarded and treasured through the seasons of her life. I'm joined by an enthralled spectator as I open Mama's ancient steamer trunk with its welter of faded stickers plastered on in dozens of bustling baggage rooms in the early gypsy years of our lives.

Ah! Here is a photograph of me at twenty-two in full rainbow pimp regalia. Slumberously evil eyes stare into the camera with an odd malevolence, perhaps due to the powerful "speed ball" (heroin and cocaine in combination) I had mainlined a half hour before I sat for the photographer.

My wee one shudders in mock repulsion at the image of the dapper predator with the insane eyes and hollers, "He ugly! He ugly!" And I feel glad that my pimp image repels her.

Here is another old group photograph of my kindergarten class, taken on the school yard with a background of blooming apple trees adazzle with snowy blossoms. On my left is a moonfaced Italian kid named Joe, my close pal. And on my right is a towering, fierce-faced, bully Polish kid with a lantern jaw thrust out, a feared enemy. That was until one soggy summer day (two, three years after the photograph) he put the strong arm on me for a bag of tootsie rolls, and in the scuffle he lumped my eye and put me to rout with tears and snot flowing.

Mama viewed my defeat and flight not only as a craven trait surfacing in her only child, but also as a symbolic transgression against and a humiliation of the whole black race. She psyched me up for victory in the return match by the simple expedient of filling me with the terror that she would murder me if I did not vanquish the bully.

She marched me toward combat and we spotted him sling-shot sniping at a pigeon with a broken wing down near the Rockford, Illinois, gas house. I saw a possible equalizer for the superior size and strength of the bully in a length of rusty pipe in the gutter. I darted for it and seized it, but Mama shook her head resolutely and unpiped me, an action which deepened my suspicion that she had gone bats.

Lantern Jaw had his usual fear-branded audience of scared kids around, and I was dizzy with fright as Mama nudged me up to the brawny kid who kept getting bigger and bigger. I was just standing there when Mama suddenly shoved me hard against the bully. He cuffed me against the side of the head; a quick look back over my shoulder at Mama's doomsday face was enough to send me into an attack orgy of rage, fear and excitement sufficient to overwhelm the bully and send him fleeing into the wind. I vividly remember that the cheers were thunderous, and so was my berserk heartbeat.

Here is one of me taken in the lap of a department store Santa Claus. Those were joyous days despite the obsessive dreaming and desiring for wondrous, impossible things that I never got—like the gentle pony, Bo Mee, with great golden-flecked eyes that I possessed and loved for so many years, in my dreams. Perhaps for me, a black kid, one reason why those days were joyous was because as a child I was not aware of this country's exclusion of most black people from the possibility of living its good life. I could still feel a pang of pride when I heard "America the Beautiful" or "The Star Spangled Banner."

Of all the horrendous maimings of the black man's psyche by America's racism, I believe it is the early crushing and destroying of this heady, vital sense of proprietary pride and emotional kinship with one's country which ranks as one of the most lamentable and disastrous.

Here is a photograph of a jet black luscious siren now known as the Black Duchess among dope dealers in the East. When she was a girl I stole her from a shoe clerk in Chicago and "turned her out." She was the Duchess of Doom for the lovesick clerk. He couldn't live without her. He blew his brains out a week after she left him. I kept her ninety-six hours. I lament that it had to be me who stole her and his life.

I'm looking now at a picture of a dear first cousin of mine taken at a bottle-covered table in a Milwaukee bar twenty years ago. She is seated with drinking buddies, her babyish face not yet hardened by whiskey and merciless life. She had musical ability but her whiskey-mauled mind suffered too much trauma too soon to allow her to use it successfully.

I looked down at her in her coffin year before last and the once softly-rounded, light tan doll was a sunken, blackened specter. Here is a yellowed half sheet of music and lyrics clipped to her picture. It was her last creative effort. It's title?—"Let's Go Get Stoned."

Here is another of ten-year-old me taken in the backyard of one of the happiest houses I have ever lived in as child or man. Henry, my stepfather, a man beautiful inside but rather odd-looking outside, lived there. And because of his presence it had to be one of the most unhappy houses Mama ever lived in.

Three white buddies are standing beside me with the summer jade glory of weeping willow trees in the background. The four of us were inseparable at school, on hiking and small game hunting trips, and in and out of one another's homes visiting and eating.

But one day in one vital and irreconcilable area of childhood activity they discriminated against me, and barred me from participation. It was spring and my fresh young heart had burst forth in goofy passion for a lispy black beauty who lived on the other side of the viaduct. My three pals and I had just had a ball dislodging rocks in my backyard and capturing garden snakes when suddenly in a mysterious manner they left me separately.

I sat alone at the edge of the backyard, idly tossing pebbles into the creek below and, perhaps turned on by the hulaing of the willows, decided to visit the lovely fox across the viaduct. It turned out that I got only a brief but prickly peek at her in a pink bathing suit as she waved and got into her father's car on the way to the beach.

As I started back across the span, I looked down absent-mindedly at the railroad cars and the wooded section along the creek. I got a flash of tow heads in triplicate amongst the trees, and decided to join my pals in whatever new adventure was about. I sneaked through the trees to surprise them. I came upon them in a little clearing. Their naked bodies were beaded from a dip in the creek as they stood in a tight circle on the bank frantically masturbating. I stayed concealed and entertained for a few moments before slipping away . . . the shocked young victim of a unique racial discrimination.

On the Fourth of July, I idly flip the television dial and am treated to an excavated spook, scripted and motivated by the mercenary medium to play his part in a patriotic "Honor America Day."

Reverend E. V. Hill, the spook, proceeds to do his thing.

He shouts into the microphones with the piercing desperation of one of the multitudes of black lynching victims in America's gory history crying out against the slicing off of his genitals, "This is my beautiful country! This is our wonderful country! America, for you we will fight and die!"

I wonder how many of the poverty-crushed members of the preacher's congregation see America through his rose-tinted nigger eyes? The preacher is succeeded by a young white woman with straw-colored hair and a wretchedly pitched voice, vapidly informing nigger me that America is great because of the vast numbers of life insurance policies in effect here, etc.

I think of the thousands of black people who don't even score for daily grits and greens, of the uncounted thousands who have been hurled into pauper ovens for cremation or piled into graves in potter's field.

Disgusted, I try the radio. The lush, mellifluous voice of a black balladeer caresses the air. The possessor of the voice, still handsome in middle age, has everything needed to join the Tom Jones and the Humperdincks in the rarified heights of a vocal super-stardom except a white face.

He is Arthur Prysock, and he is one of the many physically attractive, magnetic black male performers who have been the victims of powerful white racists in key entertainment positions and publicity media.

Only rarely does a black performer (like Harry Belafonte) with erotic radiations slip past the rules of the entertainment industry into true stardom and financial security. Those black male performers whose erotic voltage is comfortingly low, or non existent, stand a far better chance of making it big.

An even more ghastly denial is the systematic destruction of the true, vital heroes of the black race—men like Paul Robeson, Jack Johnson, W. E. B. Dubois and more recently Muhammad Ali, Huey Newton and Bobby Seale. The technique has been to deform and butcher the victim's image and character in the communications media and in the double-standard judicial slaughterhouses.

Black super-heroes of sports and entertainment (those who get the so-called universal approbation and love of white America) are valid heroes neither in spirit nor in posture, even though many unaware blacks may admire and love them as such, and envy their fortune and fame. But if we look with clear eyes at some of these usually older brothers, we see a heartbreaking portrait, as we sorrowfully realize that the brothers' very universal acceptance is, in racist America today, an indictment of their pride, integrity and black manhood.

We still love them as black brothers, but pity them for we sense that their balls were hacked off early by the brute blade of this society's unremitting oppression. These unfortunate brothers exist in a terrible psychic straitjacket of grinning, mute denial of the physical and mental atrocities inflicted upon black people in America.

White racist America hated Jack Johnson, Paul Robeson and Malcolm X. What a monstrous crime it is that the black masses did not and were not permitted to love them at least proportionately to the hatred of their white enemies.

There is a strong probability that as new young black heroes come to center stage, they will neither seek nor welcome the universal approbation and love of white America, which is tantamount, in these times, to racial treason and abdication of integrity and manhood.

The old bitter-sweet memories fall like leaves through sunshine and storm in the autumn of my life. As I face the looming, unknown winter, my mental eye peers back with remorse at the carnal ruin and sorrow of my poisonous pimp wake.

But there is solace and joy in my determination to build instead of destroy during the sunrisings left to me. I feel such pride at my survival, for the miracle is that I am not a marooned wreck on some gibbering mental reef. I am gratified to be alive at this time and place in the history of the black people's struggle. What a joyously painful transport it is to be part of that struggle, to be a besieged black man, an embattled nigger, in racist America.

THE END

This book gives amazing new information never before published in a handicapping book. It makes the whole business of winning at the races so easy, it's almost unbelievable. So easy that even if you've never bet a race before, you'll know more and win more often than any of the so-called pros. Handicapping To Win tells you how to avoid making sucker bets on sure losers; horses that are just out for exercise or are hopelessly outclassed. It tells you how to spot the horse that's out to win and how to bet these winning horses. They say "winning is everything" but this book gives you a bonus as well. It is delightful; full of racing lore and fascinating anecdotes. You'll enjoy!

HANDICAPPING TO WIN

by SCOTT FLOHR

$7.95

"Scott Flohr's new book is race track dynamite!"

■ ups your win chances by 50% ■ shows you how to make the most of post betting ■ explains how to use tote board to make more money ■ tells when class is more important than time ■ helps you spot a "fixed" race ■ saves your getting suckered by sure losers ■ gives you secret to spot those rare million dollar moves

---

ON SALE NOW AT YOUR BOOKDEALER

OR SEND MAIL ORDER DIRECT TO: **MELROSE SQUARE PUBLISHING CO., DEPT. HHP, 8060 MELROSE AVE., LOS ANGELES, CALIF. 90046**

Enclose Payment with Your Order: $7.95 (California Residents Add 5% Tax).
